Ethereal

Lizzie Collins

© Lizzie Collins 2024
All rights reserved.

All characters in this book are fictious and not intended by the author to portray persons, living or dead.

<u>For ease of reading, the names of deceased characters are underlined in the text, and the final pages contain a glossary of people and places</u>

ISBN 9798320890951

Witch Ethereal

Prologue

Who is Angela O'Connor?

Born Angela Greenwood near Beckton in Westmoreland, England Angie's great-grandmother Molly Carrick was a powerful witch from a coven in Dumfries in Scotland. She married dull Joseph Graham to escape persecution as her Wicca gifts became more apparent as she got older, and her family feared for her safety.

Molly and her husband moved right away from Scotland and bought a farm close to the small south Lakeland hamlet of Beckton, where Joseph became a successful and affluent farmer. Light-hearted Molly found him terminally boring.

They had two sons, Richard and Robert, whose characters were opposite ends of the scale. Richard was dour, aggressive and cruel and Robert, the light of his mother's life, was loving, impractical and romantic.

From jealousy, Richard loathed his brother, and after their father's death, on inheriting the farm at Bythwaite, and despite his mother's pleading, he threw Robert out to fend for himself.

The brothers had married sisters from Manchester, Claire and Moira Armstrong – Moira, the younger sister, first to Robert then a couple of years later Richard, the older brother, to Claire.

At her own sister's wedding reception, Claire fell irrevocably in love with her sister's husband and he with her. They had a long lasting and torrid covert relationship and met as often as they could at the secluded Seven Sisters stone circle, a mysterious neolithic ruin on the hills above Bythwaite.

Claire always put their uncontrollable passion down to interference from the Sisters themselves,

Claire and her husband Richard never had children, but Robert, although trying to scrape a living hill farming in Nethershaw, a market town near Kendal, had three children with his wife Moira – Ellen, Margaret and John. When John was still a newborn, their mother died of pneumonia.

Then Robert was killed in an accident on the fells and his children were left destitute. Ellen already had a job and a room in Kendal, working at the shoe factory there, and John joined the army. Both loathed the fells and never returned but Margaret, named Maggie in childhood and later Meg, aged seventeen sold the land and stock and moved to nearby Nethershaw where she was employed as a maid by the wife of the local magistrate.

Eventually, with the money she earned from the sale of her father's grazing land and stock, she bought a small allotment and began growing vegetables for sale at local markets.

Meg buckled down, and worked hard until she became the successful owner of a large arable farm and employed Dermot O'Connor as her foreman. Dermot's

Witch Ethereal

wife Deidra came to play a large part in the lives of everyone in this story.

When it came to selling the smallholding on the fells, she was contacted by her Uncle Richard's son, Joe. He gave her a very generous price for her childhood home, and together with his friend Guy Greenwood, he started a business renovating derelict fell-side properties for letting to hill-walkers.

Through Joe, Meg met his frail mother, her aunt Claire who appeared to be terrified of her husband Richard, the reason for which Meg only discovered later.

She stood up to her unpleasant uncle and eventually managed to extricate Claire from Bythwaite to her own home at Ghyll Howe near Nethershaw.

As the Wiccan strain was only transmitted through the female line, and as Molly had two sons, it missed a generation. It mostly missed Robert's children too. The only way it seemed to affect Meg's life was that she was exceptionally lucky in whatever she turned her hand to, and birds and butterflies were drawn to her like magnets.

Meg married and had a daughter Angela who, although not a witch of her great-grandmother Molly's caliber, nevertheless inherited more of her abilities than had her mother. Angela grew to adulthood living side by side with the spirits of the dead. While normal to her, it often led to unfortunate situations with the living.

This is only the very briefest of outline which leads to the beginning of the tale of Angela's life in exile and the birth of a new Circle.

Witch Ethereal

I have intentionally omitted several story lines to avoid spoilers.

Witch Ethereal

Witch Ethereal

Witch Ethereal

Chapter One

Extracting the Soul

The fresh mountain breeze pulled at my hair as I knelt on the passenger seat of Robbie's hired MG to wave goodbye to my family. We were leaving the green mountains of the English Lakes for California.

My new husband reached out a comforting hand, but I was beyond consolation. I felt as if my soul was being ripped from my chest.

My beloved mother, lonely for the two dearest friends of her life who had recently died, was now being abandoned by her only child, and my indulgent father whose heart had broken in two, waved from the yard of our farm at Scarsdale Manor. My uncle Joe and his American wife Zella – toddlers playing at their feet - stood eyes shaded against the noon-day glare.

Although they were no-longer mine to see, I knew my beloved spirits were there too to wish Robbie and me farewell. We couldn't meet again – we'd be separated not only by the Veil, but by distance and experience.

I knew we were losing not only our darling aunt <u>Claire,</u> but also Rob's desperately missed <u>mother and father,</u> and my wonderfully loving <u>Grandad Greenwood</u> who walked the pack-bridge and wheatfields by my cottage named Smyltandale – Serenity Vale in old English - by Zella. All gone forever.

Witch Ethereal

Except for <u>Molly</u> of course, my great grandmother, Wiccan extraordinaire, who stood atop the crest of Gastal fell which hid the Seven Sisters stone circle from view.

Dead close on fifty years, she was jumping up and down waving her art deco scarf, as we rounded a corner in the lane, and all I had known and loved slipped from sight.

I slid back down in my seat and Rob gave my hand a squeeze and held it over the stick-shift as he changed gear.

"Come on mate, we've a soccer team to construct or had you forgotten?"

This was part of his wedding vows. He'd married me, he insisted, so we could put together a football squad of children. I'd yet to decide if he was serious. Knowing Robbie there was little doubt he meant it. Well, pigs might fly! I wasn't losing my figure to eleven kids. I might allow two if he was lucky. Game of ping pong doubles perhaps.

All silly considerations of course, but they distracted me as was his intention. I had to try and push the past to the back of my mind and look to the future. It wasn't such a bad prospect.

Robbie and I were bound for Santa Barbara on the California coast where he had bought a holiday cottage as our permanent home. It was a holiday cottage by

American standards of course. In England it would have been a semi-palatial bungalow.

He was determined to fix it up himself. It needed quite a bit of DIY and TLC. Besides that, he'd to run his photographic studio in Santa Monica, an hour and a half away down the coast.

I was to do the interior design which would be no problem at all. Perhaps I might go and stay with my aunt Zella's former boss Nik and his wife in LA. The aunt bit was ironic since she was the same age as Rob.

Nik Chilton was a bigwig at Juno Records, and his wife Cam a world-famous jazz pianist, a beautiful, graceful woman, and my friend.

Nik had provided Rob with his first studio, and work piled in through his connections, and that of his friend Danny Charlton, international megastar whose fame was waning as he aged.

Dan, Nik, and Robbie's favorite band Lakota, had been guests at our wedding. Nethershaw would be talking for years about the hippies who desecrated their town and corrupted their children.

The truth of the matter was, one member of the band had spent nearly the entire afternoon playing 'Row, Row, Row Your Boat' with Zella and Joe's toddlers, and the lead singer of Lakota – Rick Adams - had entertained our guests for an hour with Danny. We had a free reception's show from entertainers known the world over.

It would be such a joy to be reunited with our American friends. My phantom family in Beckton and Nethershaw in Westmoreland were lost to me, so I must learn to replace them somehow. Grandad Greenwood's shade had comforted me by saying, as one circle ends another begins, and my Westmoreland circle had run its course. What form the new one would take remained to be seen.

As my Wicca gift was communicating with the souls of loved ones who had passed over, I couldn't see how this could work. I had no such people in California, it would all be new. Perhaps the closing of the circle meant I'd to begin life again with no particular gifts. I couldn't help thinking my existence would be disappointing from now on.

"Stop dwelling on the past, Anj. Wow! I can call you that all the time from now on – your mother won't be able to flatten me with her voice from across the room. Why did she hate it so much anyway?"

"Not a clue, and I'll stop brooding the minute my feet leave English soil. I promise."

Rob pulled into the car hire at Heathrow and we dropped off the MG. My husband and I were now irrevocably California-bound but my heart still ached for Scarsdale.

Chapter Two

Land of Surf and Sunshine

I dozed on the plane as the green patchwork of fields and forests slipped away below, to be replaced by clouds and black ocean.

I came round to eat, then only woke again as the plane dipped low over neatly squared industrial units and residential blocks, vegetation bleached ochre by the hot Californian sun. Here and there was a verdant square of football field or park but mostly it was drab.

Whereas I saw only despondency Robbie, once he'd disposed of his sick bag, was buzzing with the excitement of seeing his studio again and beginning work with the likes of his friends Nik Chilton and Danny Charlton.

Could we bring our opposing viewpoints together? It was going to take work and I'd no Veil family to help. Still, I wasn't about to rain on his parade.

Nik's new secretary, a plump and efficient woman called Sharon, was about as far in looks and personality from Zella as it was possible to get. Whereas Zella was lissome, softly spoken and patient, Sharon was well-rounded with an emphatic twang which spoke of her Boston upbringing.

While it was true she only got Zella's job because candidates were scarce at the time, she kept it on super-efficiency. Sharon had taken a liking to Nik which was vastly to his advantage as she was a fearsome woman.

She collected Rob and me from the airport, flinging our luggage in the boot with gusto and rattling her car keys impatiently.

"In you get..." she said, tapping her foot when we didn't move fast enough, and opening the back door as if she was a taxi driver.

Robbie turned on his sunshine and for a moment she looked about to thaw but quickly collected herself and said:

"The boss's house I've been told. Mrs. Chilton's on tour. Mr. Chilton will see to you. He's a meeting at nine so won't have long."

Apart from giving Rob a smile through clenched teeth when he turned on the charm again, that was our only conversation.

We didn't even dare to speak to each other. How she became a PA was a mystery unless it was to strong-arm the opposition into submission.

We'd left Scarsdale on a sunny lunchtime and arrived in LA to the early morning smog. Much of it would burn off as the sun rose but for now the vast parking lots which served the airport, and stretched as far as the eye could see, were engulfed in a grey shroud of dust-locked fumes. The day promised to be hot.

"It was touching on a hundred yesterday," Sharon informed us tonelessly as we pulled onto the road.

Witch Ethereal

"Oh God...," said Robin.

Sharon dropped us at the end of the drive to Nik and Cam's posh Linden Reach home. The extensive lawns were plush and green, their sprinklers humming pleasantly. The walls, decked with purple clematis and star jasmine, filled the garden with heavenly perfume.

"Not keen on those though..." said Rob, pointing out a small forest of spindly palms against the perimeter wall. "I'd root them out."

"They're a windbreak, Rob. They protect the garden from the ocean winds."

We were halfway up the drive when the door opened and a bleary-eyed Nik, still in his bathrobe, stood at the top of a flight of steps outside the front door.

"Good journey, kiddo?" he said to me, "Great to see you."

He turned to Rob, but before he could utter another word:

"Sorry Nik but I've been throwing my guts up on a plane for twenty-four hours" – slight exaggeration for effect – "and need to wash and sleep. After that... whatever floats your boat."

Nik showed us to the same room I'd used the first time I visited, when <u>Deidra</u> was at deaths door and Robbie was AWOL.

My husband took one look at the bed, collapsed upon it and was asleep as soon as his head hit the pillow.

In the cool of the evening when we'd recovered, Nik, Robin and I took a leisurely stroll through nearby Dot's as Robbie called it. To the rest of the world, it was known as the Dorothy Green Park in Santa Monica. It was an expanse of manicured green lawns edged by the Pacific Ocean and studded with palms and picnic tables, some occupied by laughing couples, some commandeered by families with small children, who splashed in nearby fountains.

We strolled along the sand to Santa Monica pier and stood to watch children build sandcastles in its shade.

The concrete pier, to a girl from Westmoreland, appeared solid and dour and a million miles away from the ornate wrought-iron counterparts which graced the sea fronts at Blackpool and Morecambe. But then those faced across the Irish Sea, and not an intimidating expanse of cruel ocean which had already flattened several predecessors.

Rob had asked if we could stay at the house in Linden Reach until he could get our home in Santa Barbara shipshape.

"Cam's back Friday," said Nik. "If you like you can stay at Linden Reach or move to the beach house where you were before. Not exactly Smyltandale, but it has its advantages."

Nik and other American friends had stayed at Scarsdale when Rob and I were married in Nethershaw, so knew my own little cottage on the riverbank there.

"Seclusion? Oh, great!" leered Robin.

Witch Ethereal

My God, he was a social disaster! Whatever was in his head came straight out of his mouth.

"You are more of a menace than the Sisters!"

Nik smiled at my embarrassment - he knew Rob of old. He also knew *our* sisters weren't the Seven Sisters studios in Hollywood.

"We'd like to stay the few days until Cam's back, then go to the beach house if that would be okay. Has Robin told you about his…our new place near Santa Barbara? Not much yet but it has great potential."

It hadn't – and never would have – the glamor of this mansion in Linden Reach but I doubted Nik and Cam would even notice.

Nik was up and away early next day, and as a visit to the Serenity Vale Studios with Robbie would entail a couple of hours conversation with Cindy, Rob's clueless receptionist, I elected to stay at Nik's and try to do something about my freckled - but pale - Westmoreland skin.

I rubbed myself well with sun-cream, lay on my stomach on the lawn and leafed through an old copy of the Orange County Magazine. It was full of articles about places I'd never heard of, with beautiful names like Capistrano and Bellflower, and articles on unknown local people, and names I recognized from Hollywood films.

One of Nik's housemaids brought me a glass of fresh orange juice. I must have slept for a little while, because by the time I picked up the glass again, the outside was frosted and the ice gone.

I'd had enough sun so showered, changed and went to explore.

I began by taking in 'Dot' as we had with Nik but walked further along to look more closely at the pier.

Its most arresting feature was a huge Ferris wheel at the end, which could be seen from fifty miles away.

I took a ride. From the top in both directions were immense swathes of sand, ant-peopled, at the ocean's edge. Mountains formed a misty backdrop in the far distance.

It wasn't Gastal Fell but it was certainly impressive. Rob had told me to look to the future so I would. With my husband's help I *would* make California my home.

Chapter Three

Lena and Back to Huntington Beach

When I picked Rob up and we drove over to lunch with Nik at Linden Reach, he was in an awful temper, such a rare thing I was startled.

Apparently, that 'twit' Cindy had done 'sod-all' since he'd left and the paperwork had piled to the ceiling in his absence.

He'd fired her, and as I was the only alternative with the experience, it looked like I had a job until he could find a suitable replacement.

I squirmed inside. What exactly did 'piled to the ceiling' mean? Robbie was sometimes prone to exaggeration. I prayed this was one of those times.

I couldn't tell if Nik was joking or not when he said:

"I can lend you Sharon for a day or two. She's very efficient."

I watched Rob's expression change from harassed to horrified.

"He couldn't do it, Nik," I said. "He doesn't have your stamina."

Me, it was then.

It wasn't so bad. Cindy had managed the telephone and appointments book, but I could only assume Rob had always done the accounting, probably taught by his mother over the years.

I'd shifted most of the work in the three days before Cam arrived home.

She looked like we had when we arrived from England – worse if anything. Her usually immaculate hair had come loose at the edges and she had bags under her eyes.

The following morning, she was up with the birds, spick and span and tossing pancakes, while one of the young servants fried bacon.

She treated me to an American hug, and I introduced her to Rob. She'd heard so much about him, she said.

"What did you hear?" said Rob, uneasily.

"We'll leave you to figure that out," said Nik.

Later that evening we left Cam to rest, moved our belongings down to their beach house, threw open the sliding door and took in great gulping gasps of sea air.

The Chilton's holiday home opened directly onto the furthest corner of Huntington Beach. The view from the deck door encompassed a vast expanse of turquoise ocean laced with surf, where it either roared or trickled to shore depending on the prevailing winds.

Robbie and I, with his mother Deidra, had stayed there when Uncle Joe had come back to California to sort out his love life, and Nik had made my husband's dreams come true by setting him up with his first professional studio.

I was sorting out the office work the next day, so went for a walk along the beach and a swim while I could.

Rob was photographing whatever took his fancy, then surprised me by putting his camera down somewhere sandless and stripping to the skin. Diving underwater through the waves, he grabbed my ankles and dragged me under the surface, holding me there for a few seconds before letting me loose to cough and splutter in the air.

"You...YOU..." was the best I could do before he wrestled me to the sand, and we made love in the waves at the ocean's edge.

After, we lay wrapped in each other's arms in the gentle swell, gazing in awe as a crimson sun sank slowly into a golden sea.

The next few days had nothing of souls or sunsets. We were at the studio so Robbie could meet up with clients and sooth any ruffled feathers caused by his absence.

The one thing I learned about the music business, and quickly, was that everything has to happen yesterday. We only slowed down when Danny Charlton dropped by, with Rick Adams from Lakota. Then Rob locked up the shop and we all went to eat shrimp at the pier.

Danny had been so kind over the intervening years since Rob had been in business. Amazingly he, and

Rob's sardonic mother <u>Deidra,</u> had discovered a real rapport in the brief time they'd known each other.

It always surprised me, renowned as Dan was, he still managed to be a normal mortal who hated salad and bit his nails.

Rick was very shy, skinny and had the faint remains of acne scars on both cheeks. A small gold cross hung from his right ear. His character was unprepossessing, but with those he knew, he was the center of any party, happy to play his guitar, and sing raucous blues whenever asked.

That Rick and Danny connected so well was probably a professional case of opposites. Danny played brilliant guitar and had a voice smooth and sweet as honey, while Rick sang like Rod Stewart but was very cool.

It didn't matter to Robbie. Dan was his friend and Rick sang lead with his favorite band. To him the arrangement was about as perfect as it could get.

Then we were back, nose to the grindstone, at Rob's Third Street studio in Santa Monica, and he was giving a tight-lipped Jeeves impression to various pompous twits in weird clothes.

On the few occasions I wasn't needed, I spent time with Cam when she was available. Usually, we sat about gossiping and drinking coffee. Occasionally we ate lunch with some of her friends and colleagues.

I manage to fit in with most people in new company, but when Cam introduced me to one particular woman, whose hand I shook, I got a distinctly uneasy feeling. This was something I hadn't felt since I'd left Westmoreland, and it seemed at odds with sunny southern California. The woman's name I learned was Lena Michaels.

It was just a vague feeling but enough to make me take careful note of her as we drank our wine. She seemed nervous and drank more than perhaps was wise, then left early.

"She suffers from migraine," said Cam.

Chapter Four

Reina del Sur

Other diners were enjoying the sunshine on a flower-decked garden terrace. There was a soft buzz of conversation, and prim waitresses moved silently between the tables. When we finished lunch, we went our separate ways.

Cam dropped me off at Third Street and I picked up the phone which was ringing as I went in. It was another shoot referral from Nik's office.

Rob was getting snowed under. He really had to think of employing an assistant. The trouble was, he had such exacting standards it was going to be difficult to find someone suitable who would take the money he was prepared to offer. He'd have to pay more and make less profit.

He didn't quite see it that way. Apparently, he had a ten-year plan which included property, soccer teams, profits and travel.

Currently, profit was heading the list because he wanted a small fortune to put the Santa Barbara house to rights. Make-do wasn't good enough for his Princess. That was me. When I pointed out I was a farm worker from Westmoreland he simply said I'd been upgraded.

Increasingly, Rob would make a window in his work schedule and disappear, leaving me in charge of the office while he went somewhere he refused point blank to discuss. I was itching with curiosity which only got worse by the week.

"I'm beginning to think you have another woman stashed away somewhere, O'Connor," I said one day when he'd pushed me to the limit.

"You know I adore you, babe. Besides which we've a football team to start."

"Well, you'd better sit down because the center-forward's on his way."

I'd never seen him lost for words. He was totally gobsmacked.

"Here, sit down," I said, thinking the roles should be reversed. Shouldn't the pregnant woman get the chair?

I brought him water from the cooler.

"Are you alright? I know it must have come as a surprise but…"

"Surprise? You have to be putting me on. It's bloody Krakatoa!"

He had a thing for volcanos. My engagement ring he'd dubbed Kilimanjaro.

"It might be a girl. Then we'd have to start again," Rob said with a wicked grin.

He grabbed his jacket and me, dashed to the door and locked up the studio. In the middle of the day too, which was unheard of.

Despite his commitment to frugality, the car he handed me into as if I was made of glass, was a brand-new Corvette in ghastly yellow.

He totally ignored me for a full half hour as we drove down the freeway in silence. I'd thought the conception of his firstborn might elicit a bit more excitement than that.

But then my thoughts were taken up with wondering where we were going. I'd assumed it'd be so he could show me what he'd done to the Santa Barbara house, but we were travelling south, parallel with the coastline. We skirted the landward side of Marina del Rey with its huge luxury yachts with forest of masts, and bypassed the airport. Then endless rows of identical bungalows dotted with wilted trees and parched grass back and front, lined the road on either side.

"Where the hell are we going, Robbie. I've never seen anywhere quite like this."

"I know. It's worse than the Mojave."

Eventually the suburban sprawl gave way to the smart suburb of Torrance, its green streets lined with coast oaks, their branches impossibly twisted, and banks of succulents interspersed with brilliant poppies.

Emerald lawns fronted low white walls, and waterfalls of wisteria tumbled from gutter and gable.

Rob pulled up in front of a smart house, blindingly white, and tile-trimmed in the Spanish style.

"Just got to pop in here for a minute. Won't be long."

Witch Ethereal

He ran up a flight of shallow steps lined with tubs of bright azaleas.

Within a couple of minutes, he returned and beckoned me inside.

"C'mon – the owner wants to say hello."

Who could it be? Not Rick Adams that was for sure. This kind of smart residence wasn't his style at all. Danny? Could be. Rob had an increasing number of wealthy clients in the music industry, and recently he'd signed up a couple of Hollywood A-listers. It could have been any one of them – they were all as rich as Croesus.

I climbed the steps into a large entrance hall with an opulent crystal chandelier. A double staircase led to an upper floor, with an enormous oval mirror on the landing where the flights met. Beneath it was a Louis Quinze style hall table, with a spray of roses in a crystal vase.

I'd never seen anything quite so opulent.

"Pretty, isn't it?" said Rob. "Come and meet the owner."

He fairly bounded up the lefthand flight of stairs and stood by the table, waiting for me to catch up.

That chandelier was gorgeous. It's drops caught the light in a myriad rainbows. I stood on the stairs to admire it.

"Come on!" said Rob, grabbing my hand and pulling me up the last half-dozen steps. "They'll be sick of waiting."

I stood beside him on the landing and he bent and kissed me lingeringly on the lips, before gently twisting my head towards the mirror.

"Welcome to 214 Ocean Ridge Drive, my darling," he said, kissing my cheek. "Meet the new owner."

His eyes shone with such affection and pride, I said:

"Goddamn, Robin O'Connor. What have you done?"

He sat on the top step and laughed until tears ran down his face.

"Nik told me you'd never believe it! I owe him fifty bucks. I said you would."

He went off into further peals of mirth.

"So, who does it belong to, you…you…?"

Words failed me.

He grabbed my hand again, dragged me back to the mirror and dropped a bunch of keys in my hand.

"It's yours. Call it an early birthday present."

I still thought he was making fun of me, until he opened the drawer in the little table and pulled out a manilla envelope.

The deeds were made out in the name of Mrs. Angela O'Connor. He hadn't even included himself.

"We can't afford this!" I said, my brain cells still not fully connecting.

"That's something else we need to talk about," he said. Then: "I thought we might christen the house 'Reina del Sur'. That's Queen of the South in Spanish – best I could think of for a football club."

"It's also the affectionate name given to Dumfries where <u>Molly</u> was born." I mused.

Chapter Five

Admissions

Rob held back while I wandered around the house. It was partially furnished but needed softening with rugs, cushions and knick-knacks. It needed personalizing.

After the knock-me-down-dead impression of the entrance, the rooms were quite small. It made them look cozier.

The main guest bedroom had a whole wall of blinds, and a sliding door which opened onto the tiling around a small pool.

It was perfect. Now, how had he paid for it? Had he robbed a bank as Deidra often feared?

Back at the beach house, Rob poured me a large glass of red and sat across the table leafing through a sheaf of papers, sorting them into order.

"Right," he said, "We've been married for some time now and without the aid of stones or mothers, I've confessions to make."

He handed over the top three sheets and watched the expression on my face closely. They were a bank statement for his studio in Santa Monica.

"Read it," he said.

I ran my finger down the figures of the first sheet, then the others. They were substantial but not Reina del Sur healthy.

"So?"

He handed over a slightly thicker wad of papers headed Serenity Vale Studios Inc, Lake Avenue, Pasadena.

I stared at the total in disbelief. The bottom line was eight digits long.

He removed the statement from the table - I'd dropped it in shock - and replaced it with the remaining sheets, which were headed Smyltandale Photographics Inc, Huntington Beach. The total was astronomic.

"Oh, yeah! Where'd you have these printed? Ha ha... very funny!"

"Nope," he said seriously, shaking his head. Real McCoy. See... the paper's watermarked."

Momentarily the whole world stood still and I gazed at him in stunned silence, then I must have bolted down the beach, because the next thing I remembered was sitting shaking, my back against a piling of the pier, and my bottom on puddled sand.

Robbie – ROBBIE O'CONNOR! My husband...was... No. He must be in league with the Mafia – or worse, some drug cartel using studios as a front. ROBBIE? No.

Rob arrived puffing and panting and took a moment or two of deep gasping to compose himself.

"What have you done, Rob?" I said, standing and backing behind the post as if he was about to smack me in the mouth.

"See? I knew you'd do this! That's why I kept quiet. It wasn't until you told me about Stanley Matthews, I needed to do something about it."

"Are you telling me you otherwise wouldn't have bothered saying anything at all?"

"Come on... you must have had some idea. Where did you think I went to when I disappeared? Palisades Park?"

"The answer to that has to be a big fat YES! All your life you've avoided responsibility. How the hell would I know where you were?" I said, "Who the hell are you anyway?"

I turned and walked under the pier and down the beach.

"Your bum's wet, did you know?" he said, following.

I rounded on him irate and slapped his face. He stopped dead in his tracks.

"Does that mean you don't want me anymore?" he said, and a lone tear rolled down his cheek. "I'm sorry if I did the wrong thing. Please don't leave."

Whoever thought a millionaire could be so pathetic!

"Come on – you can buy me a burger," I said, relenting.

"Might just about manage it."

He scrabbled around in his pockets and pulled out a few dollar bills. I punched him in the chest.

"But I do like the house – I won't send it back, I promise."

His grin was back, broader than ever.

"Knew you wouldn't."

We went to a place on Ocean Avenue just across from the pier.

"You do realize it'll take me a while to get my head round this, don't you?"

"Would it help if I gave you accounts to do? That always settled Ma."

A man behind Rob sat clumsily on the edge of his chair, and it tipped sideways depositing him on the floor. I grinned over Rob's shoulder.

He swiveled round in alarm,

"Jeez, don't tell me it's started again. Who're the spooks this time - Elvis? Buddy Holly?"

"No some bloke just landed on his ass."

We went back to the beach house and sat on the decking.

Neither of us spoke for quite a while but just gazed out across the ocean's expanse, each trying to come to terms with their own demons. Rob broke the silence:

"Does it upset you not seeing dead people anymore? Have you noticed anything here?"

"No. I met one of Cam's friends called Lena who gave me the heebie-jeebies, but I don't think she was dead because she was knocking back the vino like you wouldn't believe. It gave her a headache and she left."

I walked to the water's edge and dabbled my feet in the ocean, examining the ripples in the sand.

"Why did you do it Rob? We're supposed to be partners in life. Why wouldn't you let me in?"

"I'm not entirely sure. I just wanted to give you the whole world, so you'd believe how much I loved you, I guess.

"Those bloody Stones kept getting in the way. You thought it was them, not me. Then my mother kicked me out until I'd made something of myself – I nearly missed her passing because of it. If it hadn't been for you, I wouldn't have been there at the end. Thank you, Angela."

He held my gaze and whispered ardently:

"I really do thank you with all my heart."

He kissed my palm.

"Well… there's no undoing it now. Thanks to you and my mother, for better or worse I'm a success.

"Despite the playacting about not being able to pay wages, I do have some pretty good staff. I'll take you to meet them when you're looking less harassed."

Chapter Six

Start From the Beginning

I woke early the next morning feeling decidedly queasy. Robin wasn't there which was perhaps as well, as I spent the next ten minutes in the bathroom examining the bottom of the toilet.

I found him, a seated silhouette against the ocean, his toes in the water. He was lobbing pebbles he'd collected in a small heap, into the gentle surf and gazing unseeing into a glorious sunrise.

"Did you know you were at your loveliest when your eyes are heavy with sleep and your hair is tousled," he whispered without looking at me. "That's why I drew your portrait that day at the Seven Sisters – the one your Dad put over the mantle at Scarsdale."

His expression didn't alter, but he said:

"You didn't want it."

I'd gone from loving him to wishing I was dead in the blink of an eye.

"I hadn't yet admitted to myself you were the love of my life. I thought you were my best friend and the Sisters were to blame for your feelings. I thought you'd get over it."

He put his arm around me and kissed my hair.

"I hadn't realized until now, you were as thick as I was. It's a wonder we ended up together at all.

"I think we need to go back to England. Just for a little while," he reflected. "We need time and distance to think."

He did look drawn and tired. I had a mental image of a time long ago when I'd found him on the riverbank at Ghyll Howe, hanging upside-down from a branch, to get a shot of a nest full of baby blackbirds. Where had that carefree spirit gone? Had I done this to him?

"Don't be sad, my darling – you're right. We need some perspective," I agreed.

"Do you realize that's the first time you've ever called me darling?"

Rob needed to get his affairs in order before we could leave. Pasadena and Huntington studios pretty much ran themselves, but he'd been dealing with the Santa Monica business personally since he first left Juno Records, so he'd to find someone to put in charge.

It was over a month before Robin was finally ready, by which time Stanley was earning his first division status. 'He' could kick like a mule.

"We need to get a move on Robbie," I said, when preparations were taking longer than expected, "or your emergency might not be imagined."

A thought struck him.

"What nationality can a child born in mid-air between two countries claim? Is it where the plane comes from…or the nationality of the parents? What if the dad's from Italy and the Mother from Poland? Would it be Italopolski?"

"I take it these are rhetorical questions?"

Rob had hoped he might introduce me to his staff before we left, but there just wasn't time. I briefly met his stand-in at Santa Monica. Don Fargo was Alan Dean's undermanager at the Pasadena studio and came highly recommended. I think Robbie was intending to make the position permanent if he had the makings of a manager. Being a gifted photographer doesn't always translate into man-management and financial skills. Still, Al spoke well of him and Rob trusted his word.

I rang my mother and asked her to fix up Smyltandale for two and a half O'Connors. We'd be there within the month. The silence at the other end of the line was deafening, so I put the receiver down. Plenty of time for hysterics later.

Once we were onboard the plane and I'd managed to stretch the seatbelt over the bump, we were off.

He spent the entire flight with his hand on my belly, making sure the baby kept kicking, 'just in case of emergencies'. I wasn't entirely sure what he thought they might be, or what he could do about them hundreds of feet in the air with no doctor and a flight attendant trained in first aid. He was so preoccupied he didn't even turn green although he was very pale through his tan.

Witch Ethereal

I was so excited at the prospect of seeing everyone again – this side of the Veil and I hoped at least one or two from the other – I couldn't settle to reading the book I'd brought or watching some second-rate B-movie. I jiggled about in my seat until Rob couldn't tell which was me, and which was baby.

We were only just on speaking terms by the time we landed and picked up the luggage.

"I'm sorry," he said, "I've never been a Dad before. I don't know what to do."

"And you think I do? Your bit's done – mine's still to come and I'm terrified. What if I do it wrong?"

"You can't give birth wrong. Women have been doing it for a million years and getting it right. What makes you any different?"

I huffed and waddled off to the car hire. He'd no bloody clue.

Mum had rung a couple of times since I'd told her about the baby. Was I the only one excited about this? Rob had turned into Dr Spock and never shut up with the advice, and my mother kept telling me it hurt, and I should put my feet up because my ankles would swell. I didn't need anyone to tell me that.

I could only assume no-one had told my Dad. It was going to be excruciating. I just prayed Joe would maintain his usual *sangfroid* and Zella's recent experience with babies would make her of use – otherwise I was scuppered.

Witch Ethereal

We were just about level with Harrogate when my waters broke. I'd forgotten that bit.

Chapter Seven

The Forward Centre-Forward

Rob was absolutely no bloody use at all. He pulled into a gas station, panicked and yelled: "He's not due for another month – will he make it? Hell – will *I* make it?"

"Get inside and ring for an ambulance," I yelled, and when he hesitated, "NOW – not next goddamn week."

He bumbled about a bit then dashed to the pay booth and flailed his arms about, until the guy behind the desk got the message and picked up the phone.

Anastasia Deidra O'Connor was born at six-thirty-seven on the evening of August twenty-first in the maternity ward of Keighley Hospital. She weighed five pounds four ounces and didn't make a squeak for twenty-four hours until the mid-wife gave her a hefty thwack. Then she didn't stop for the next six months. I'd pretty soon found out why it is women have the babies. Men would die of heart failure – epidural would become flavor of the month.

Early the following morning after I'd been resettled on the ward and had some sleep, Mum, Dad, Joe, Zella – sans kids - Sean and Paul – sans families, turned up. They were let in two at a time by a Rosa Kleb of a ward sister who also took them to the nursery to see the new family member – the only one asleep amongst a whole host of wailing newborns.

"Is there something wrong with her?" my Dad demanded of Rosa.

"Nope..." she said. "Fit as a fiddle. Bit on the small side but she'll soon catch up."

Rob demanded, and got, an ambulance to take me to Kendal hospital after three days. I'd another couple of days there, then we were whisked off to Scarsdale, where I had to virtually fight Rob, aided and abetted by my Dad, to get out of bed.

Anastasia was bottle-fed from the start, mostly because her Dad wouldn't put her down long enough for breast feeding. He was a nightmare. He called her Stan.

"Funny name," said my Dad. "Where'd that come from?"

"Don't ask," I said, glaring at Robbie, who jiggled his daughter and stuck the bottle back in her questing mouth.

"She was going to be a center-forward but she was the wrong sex," he said, as if that cleared everything up.

My Dad looked completely bemused – as he would, of course.

"She's one hundred per cent English!" crowed my mother when there were only us Greenwoods and American O'Connors remaining. "Mum and Dad English, born in England – and a witch."

Robbie's head snapped up. That hadn't occurred to him.

"Maybe it'll pass her by too," he said hopefully, but without conviction. "She'll grow up in Torrance and get an American education."

I couldn't see how that mattered – a witch was a witch was a witch. She'd just sing the Star-Spangled Banner instead of God Save the Queen.

Anastasia giggled a gurgle in her dad's face and threw up on his shirt. He didn't seem to notice but put down the bottle and put her over his shoulder to rub her back. She decorated the back of his shirt in like manner.

Robbie was besotted. He walked around smelling of baby sick until Mum complained and grabbed his daughter so he could go and change.

Between them, I'd managed to hold my daughter for less than an hour since she was born. She'd made an excellent first impression. At three weeks old she'd put her Dad in his place in no uncertain terms, and caused an argument between him and her Grandma. I foresaw a great future for her.

Robbie had to go back home early because of work, but he insisted I stay behind for a few weeks until I got my strength back and Anastasia was fit for the journey.

I'd miss him of course, but I couldn't in all honesty say I was sorry. It would be good to spend some alone time with my Mum and Dad. We could catch up and they could get to know the baby before we went back.

"Deidra'd be proud of Rob," said my mother, over breakfast. "California's been good for him. He looks healthy, and neat and tidy for a change."

Just how was I to tell her about Reina del Sur. It would have to be broached sooner or later.

"Do you think I should take Anastasia to the Stones to see if <u>Molly</u> turns up? <u>Grandad Josh</u> said I'd finished this Circle and wouldn't see them again. I'm not sure what that means. What do you think, Mum?"

"Don't know, but <u>Molly</u>'s not one for keeping to the rules. Give it a shot.

"You're going to have to do something about that child's name," she said, changing tack, "I can't shout 'Anastasia, muck out the pens, or Anastasia, put a sock in it! She sounds like a Russian Princess, and Deidra's not here to keep her feet on the ground. Whatever possessed you to choose such a foreign name?"

"Robbie wanted to call his son Stanley Matthews after the footballer. No idea why. He doesn't even like football."

"Oh, never mind. It's Robbie so the reasons are probably beyond my understanding. How about we call her Anna? No way on earth am I calling her Stan."

So, Anna it was. Except for her Dad.

A week later I swaddled my little girl in a cellular blanket against a sharp September breeze, and Mum ran us to see Zella and Uncle Joe at Bythwaite. The uphill walk to the Sisters was shorter from there and avoided the scree slope on the Scarsdale side of the ridge.

Witch Ethereal

I felt very guilty as I climbed over the style and began to cross the pastures. I knew Rob would hate me doing this.

He'd accepted I'd regularly had dealings with our aunt Claire, but was dubious about the rest. I would tell him what I'd done, but later…much later. Preferably even later than that.

Anna woke and began to whitter uneasily. Perhaps she sensed what was happening, perhaps she could feel the pull of the Stones. I stuck her dummy in her mouth and she went back to sleep.

I'd no confidence at all Molly'd be there, and I was proved right. She wasn't, although we waited nearly an hour. When I feared the baby might get cold, I went back to Bythwaite, but I promised myself I'd try again before I'd to go home.

That evening Dad was back early, so I decided to tackle our financial standing in California. It was worse than owning up to destitution.

"Robbie's done quite well in Orange County – that's the area we live in – he now has three studios. He's worked unbelievably hard."

"Well, that's a turn up for the books," said my Mum. "Whoever would have thought it? I did wonder, when you got married, if we'd be bailing you out of a Victorian garret at some point. I'm glad he's lived up to his responsibilities."

Anticipating this conversation, I'd thought to bring some proof - the statements Robin had shown me. I put them on the table and went to give Anna her bottle – the coward's way out."

My Dad strode into my room ten minutes later, white with rage and shaking a wad of papers in his clenched fist.

"What the fuck, Angela. What in God's name is this pile of crap? No wonder that bastard disappeared back to America in a cloud of dust. How the hell did he manage to borrow this? Joe and I haven't seen a penny back from him from…the first time!"

Mum entered my room at that point because Anna was yowling like a stuck pig. Over the screams she yelled at my Dad:

"I don't suppose it's occurred to you it might be true?" then… "Shut that bloody brat up Angela, before I strangle it!"

Very grandmotherly.

I pushed the pair of them out of the room and did my best to settle an irate baby back to sleep.

Chapter Eight
Molly Meets Anna, Back to Reina del Sur

I went into Nethershaw with Mum a time or two, but there was no sign of my dead people. I hadn't really been expecting them, so although I was saddened, I wasn't disappointed.

I also went back to the Sisters on the off-chance Molly might have the stamina to spare me some time. Besides, I wanted her to meet Anna.

There was no way of inviting her to the Stones, but over the years I'd become well-aware that the dead sometimes knew when they were needed. Often, they knew more than I did, as when they shoved me in Rob's direction. It drove me mad at the time and took real guts on my part to admit they were right and I was wrong – especially since it gave Robin the chance to claim both dead and alive were routing for him.

It seemed Molly had tuned into my thoughts, because when I carried Anna one last time to the Sisters before I'd to pack and leave, she was sitting on top of her own stone, looking like a teenager and swinging her legs.

I prayed for strength. If a mature Molly was hard to deal with, her younger self was impossibly cheeky and unhelpful. However, this time she surprised me.

"Hello, Molly," I said, hoping for the best, "I've brought someone to meet you."

"Ooo, Anastasia – how wonderful. Stick her on top of my grave and I'll take a look."

Ewk!

"We call her Anna – at least I do. I'll put her over here if you don't mind. Graves are for dead people."

"Have it your own way," she said sulkily.

I unwrapped Anna from her outer blanket, spread it on the ground and placed her on it.

She whinged crossly until she saw Molly peeking over my shoulder. Anna was still only a few weeks old and should have been too young to focus her gaze properly, but when she saw Molly – zap! – there was no doubt whatever she'd seen her. Her eyes were fixed on her great-great grandmother's, and her face was wreathed in smiles.

She twiddled her toes and giggled.

Molly reached down to tickle her, realized she was on the wrong side of the Veil and swore loudly.

"Damn and blast!" she frowned, "There are some disadvantages to being dead! Never mind, there are advantages too. Put her where I told you in the first place."

I did as I was told this time, mostly because I was intrigued that my six-week-old daughter could actually see Molly at all.

I laid her gently down on the grave mound.

"Unwrap her – all the way down to the skin," ordered Molly.

"I can't do that - she'll freeze."

"Don't be silly. She's a witch. I doubt she'll even notice."

"I'm a witch, and I do," I said, thoroughly annoyed, "what makes you think she won't?"

"Because she's a Coven witch. Probably more powerful than me. You saw how she connected with me."

"She hasn't been initiated – how could she be?"

"Coven witches are born, but if they're initiated, they can all draw on each other's powers. You can see and communicate with the dead, I can travel and appear at will."

"I'm not a Coven witch then?"

"No. You can't link and Anna can. Didn't you notice what happened when she met another Coven witch? She recognized me straight away, and in her mind she called me Molly – I heard her quite distinctly.

"You'll have to keep a close eye on her when she's small. Her magic will be all over the place until she learns to control it. Don't let her burn the house down or throw Robin down the stairs when he's ticked her off.

"I'll help when I can, but it's better she doesn't see me again until she comes into her power. That way I can keep a covert eye on her. I'll make sure she hears me though – don't worry your head about that."

"Oh hell! Life's not going to be worth living from now on."

"Only for about the first ten years – then she'll have it under control."

"TEN YEARS?"

She shrugged:

"You have a very special child here. Guard her well."

Grandad Greenwood's words came back to mind:

"The Graham circle has closed and a new one must begin. Your future lies in California."

"If I have more babies, will they be witches like Anna?"

"The bloodline protects itself. She will probably be the only girl."

"That'll please Robbie," I grinned, "He wants a soccer team of boys."

"It wouldn't take a witch to understand how unlikely *that* is. Wrap her up and take her home. I'll see you…when I see you, I suppose," she said as she sank gracefully to the ground in a haze of mist.

Anna screamed – for about half an hour without stopping to draw breath.

Ten years! And I'd to break to Rob there were now two weirdos in the O'Connor California tribe – he was outnumbered.

On the way out, I was waddling with baby, on the way back I was bowed down with made-up bottles of formula, changes of baby clothing and diapers, bags for in case I needed to dispose of anything. My own stuff was minimal – it had to be.

Dad carried my bags as far as he could, then I was blessed to find a member of the on-board staff who helped me get to my seat and stow all my crap underneath.

Thankfully, flights to LA from London were now non-stop, or I had no idea how I'd have coped.

Rob ran to meet me at the passport desk and took the bags. He looked dapper, relaxed and smelled of Eau Sauvage. I looked like a panicky train-wreck and smelled of baby sick.

Ignoring me totally, he took hold of his daughter, who although having created havoc for most of the journey, smiled and cooed up at him as if he was the center of her Universe. I was looking forward to telling him why her eyes focused and why she could lovingly pat his cheek at little more than six weeks old.

"Hello chicks! How's my baby girl?"

He picked Anna up, tossed her unbelievably high in the air, caught her deftly then nuzzled her neck. She giggled then spoilt the whole thing by throwing up on his expensive shirt.

"Hello, light of my life," he said, finally acknowledging my existence. "You look a bit of a wreck."

I would be sending him, on his own with Anna, on a trip to visit her grandparents at the first opportunity, while I sunned myself in the pool and swigged Champagne.

Witch Ethereal

Robbie snagged a passing air stewardess, plonked Anna in her arms, swiveled me around and kissed me like Valentino. He thanked the stewardess very much, took his daughter and trollied us to the baggage pickup and parking lot.

We were back at Reina del Sur in less than an hour.

We had a small sundeck on the house roof. It wasn't much used, since we sat round the pool, but it had a superb view right down to the ocean at Redondo Beach, with its splendid pier, weekly farmer's market and outdoor cinema screen. Anna would truly grow up in a land of milk and honey – or as she knew it by the time she was six months old, chocolate.

Rob held her up in the air and moved her round so she could see the city lights.

"This is your home, sweetheart. I love you."

Robbie, who had taken every book on childcare from the three public libraries in Torrance, lolled naked at the poolside, engrossed in articles such as 'Why you shouldn't feed chocolate to children under twelve months.' – bit late for that – and 'Why you should always dispose of diapers double-wrapped."

He was an expert. He told me so. Frequently.

Chapter Nine

A Gift for Daddy

We were content to learn how to be a family for a few more months. Anna was early crawling – six months – and had managed 'Dada' by seven months, mainly because Rob, when at home, spent her every waking moment repeating that one word over and over.

Oddly, her next word sounded like Mol, which she hadn't been taught. Nonetheless, she'd sit chewing a wet comfort-blanket, propped up with cushions on the couch, chuntering to herself and laughing.

"I know. I'll help you pack Stan's stuff and we'll go up to Santa Barbara and see what there's left to do. What do you say?" suggested Rob.

"Fine - apart from the fact your daughter's name's Anna."

"Told you that, did she? Funny she should tell you one thing and me another."

For a moment he pretended to look puzzled, then shrugged and started stuffing things any old how into a canvas shoulder-bag.

Since the conversation with Molly, I confess I did watch Anna carefully. What if she did burn the house down? The throwing of Rob down the stairs was less likely since he never told her off.

That apart, I was fascinated to know what gifts she'd acquired. Molly had said most witches only had one skill, but as head of a Coven, her powers were drawn from the others in her Circle. Anna didn't have a Circle, but that she had more than one gift very quickly became obvious.

Young as she was, some were becoming slowly apparent. She appeared to be able to communicate without speech, particularly with animals and birds. But as yet, these were suspicions.

Rob hadn't bothered much with the Santa Barbara property since Reina del Sur.

By comparison it looked tatty. I'd been too distracted by Robbie to notice its faults the one and only other time I'd seen it. There was thick dust on top of the aircon, and a loose wire hanging out at the side which Rob hadn't got round to fixing. There was a crack in one of our en-suite floor tiles, and as the house had been standing empty, the garden was non-existent, its grass dead and bleached by the sun.

We spent quite a while looking round. Rob thought it would be good to let it as a holiday home. It'd give me something to do, he said, while he was out at work. I was stunned he thought I might get bored with a baby to look after.

"Get a nanny," Rob said. "Perhaps you could do some accounts at home then…"

That sounded very thoughtless but in truth his intentions were entirely honorable. He wanted to lighten my workload but then he wasn't yet aware of what Anna may be capable of. He thought she was human like him.

Of course she was human, but nothing like him at all.

It was at that precise moment he realized Anna was missing. We both panicked and ran round the house like lunatics calling her name. She seemed to have disappeared into thin air.

Robbie lost it completely. It was I who took control.

"Take some deep breaths and calm down. She can't be far. If she's not in the house she must be in the garden."

"The garden's open-plan – she could be halfway to Santa Barbara by now."

"Not on her hands and knees she couldn't. Stop being hysterical and think."

He dashed out onto the road which thankfully was empty, and finally found her. She'd crawled into next door's garden and was totally absorbed scratching in the soil with a stick.

When I caught up to Rob, he was holding Anna in his arms. He must have been gripping her too tightly because she was whacking him over the head with her stick and shouting 'Daddy' at the top of her voice.

He didn't notice he was no longer Dada. but when he put her down, she grabbed my jeans, and pulled herself upright. She was just about twelve months old. Rob thought he had the cleverest child in the world. It never occurred to him she was as weird – creepier even – than her mother. He'd thought, God bless him in his naivety, we'd left the witchy thing back in Scarsdale.

Witch Ethereal

I turned to pick Anna up and glanced where she'd been scratching away at the soil. The dead turf around the hole had turned brilliant green, fading outwards to the ochre of the dead grass, and the sad buds on an overhanging oleander had become lush, and as I looked, one popped open and its satin petals unfurled.

Robbie was so cock-a-hoop to have found Anna again, all he noticed was she was black-bright and needed a bath.

I left him to it and dashed back next door, just to make sure I hadn't been seeing things. I hadn't. The green had spread a little further outward, and several more buds had come to life. It had stopped there, but then she was just a year old. She might be rejuvenating the Mojave by the time she was ten.

When Rob was at work, one bright and breezy day about twelve months later, I packed up a bucket and spade, and with towels and sun cream headed out to the beach. Hopefully my daughter would be a normal child when distracted by sea, sun and sand.

Anna was busily engaged in bashing hell out of a sandcastle with her spade. Lulled by the sound of surf and the cry of overhead birds, I closed my eyes in relaxation for just a moment. But it must have been longer because when I shook myself awake, Anna was missing.

I just caught sight of the tail end of her as she disappeared onto the boardwalk.

I ran like hell, but it was clear she was going to get to the road before me. I was sobbing and calling her name, but when I got to the edge of the sand, I could hardly believe my eyes.

At two years old, she was crouching on the ground in front of a taxicab with her hand held out in a 'stop' gesture. With the utmost concentration she'd picked up a small but terrified tabby kitten which had been caught in the traffic.

"Daddy," she said determinedly.

How the hell would I explain *that* to him. I'd no confidence at all she wouldn't break into a highly articulate explanation as to why Momma had let her run into the middle of a busy road so she could rescue a cat! She'd probably be able to do it in French and Spanish as well.

When Molly said I'd to watch her carefully she wasn't kidding. I was sure even she hadn't had in mind stopping traffic on the seafront in Santa Barbara in her third year.

Oh God, only another eight to go.

Chapter Ten

The Confession

That evening, when Anna was washed, smelled sweetly of baby powder and was unconscious enough not to cause World War Three, I decided Rob had to know.

He'd accepted the kitten seriously from an obviously delighted daughter, and at present it was curled up in her crib. Wasn't there supposed to be an affinity between witches and cats? I'd never felt any particular draw myself.

It wasn't that I hadn't been expecting these developments – it was just how much and how quickly it was all happening. I needed Rob's help desperately. Hopefully, he'd had enough practice with *me* not to completely freak with what I was about to say.

I went to make a cup of tea, and when I returned the poor soul, tired out by a hard day's work, had fallen asleep in front of the TV.

Putting the tray down on the coffee table, I gave him a vigorous shake, then sat beside him and cuddled under his arm, gripping it so he couldn't bolt:

"I have something to tell you Robbie, and you're going to hate me for it."

"That's what you said before you admitted you're a weirdo and I nearly had a heart-attack," he laughed.

"Yes, but this is worse – much worse – and I don't have your mother to frighten you into sanity."

He started to flick through the TV channels.

"Couldn't be worse. What other lunatic claims to see dead people? The only thing worse than that, would be claiming Stan was the same."

"Anna – and she is."

He took a sip of tea and grinned.

"Had me going there for a minute."

Perhaps he couldn't hit the roof if I sat on his knee I thought without much confidence, but I sat on his knee anyway.

As usual when I cuddled up to him, he started to pepper me with kisses to distract me. Now had to be the time so I got off his knee sharpish and sat back beside him instead.

"Before I brought Anna back from Scarsdale, I took her to see Mol…"

"You did WHAT?"

"I knew you wouldn't like it, but it had to be done. Anna was only weeks old, but when she saw Molly, her eyes focused and she held out her arms to her.

"Molly told me things I never would have known."

"Molly should learn to keep her trap shut! What am I saying? Molly's been dead for decades."

"You sound just like Uncle Joe. Don't be daft – shutting your ears won't make it go away. You have to understand that not only is she a witch…"

He'd gone a funny color – puce and white in patches.

"…not only is she a witch, she's a Coven witch like <u>Molly</u>. In other words, a super-witch. <u>Molly</u> warned me it might take ten years for her to learn to control her magic so we have to be vigilant. I need you to help me, Rob. I can't do this alone."

He began to hyperventilate, so I handed him his tea and sat back to wait.

"Do you believe her?" eventually he asked weakly, which was daft because I clearly did.

"After this afternoon I have to. I'd have spared you all this if I could."

"The only thing to happen this afternoon was the kitten she found. It was the best gift she could have given me – she shared something she loved."

"She did. But you don't know how she got it."

I recounted the afternoon's happenings including my shame at having fallen asleep when I should have been watching her.

He looked horrified, which of course he'd every right to.

"By the time I caught up with her she was halfway across the road…"

"You stupid… you could have killed my daughter!"

He jumped to his feet but I was too annoyed at the 'my', not 'our', to care.

"Oh, sit down and stop being such a drama queen!"

But he didn't – he left. For four hours.

I went to lay on the bed, pulling Anna's crib up close. She must have picked up on the bad feeling because she whittered continuously until Rob came back. The cat snoozed on, undisturbed.

I'd expected Rob to reek of beer but he didn't. It was clear he'd walked for miles though, because he was exhausted and had a haunted look I'd never seen before.

He appeared worse than when his mother died. There would be no way I could fix this. I just had to help him understand. He looked so beaten but I had to finish the tale of the cat.

"Anna was crouched in the middle of a busy road. She'd her hand out stopping the traffic and picked the kitten up. It surely would have been run over if she hadn't."

"And did it occur to you *she* might have died?"

"You know, it actually didn't. Once I saw her with her hand out and the calm tenderness with which she picked up the kitten, I had no doubt at all she was safe."

Rob gave Anna her bottle before laying her down to sleep then came to bed. He stared at the ceiling, not touching me. I turned on my side and rocked the cradle gently. Our daughter slept on; the cat yawned and rearranged itself with its paw across her chest.

I tried to sleep but the air was so charged it was impossible.

Witch Ethereal

Rob got up and walked up the stairs to the sun terrace. When I looked in an hour later he was sitting, still naked and with bowed head, as the first of the dawn rays rose above the horizon.

I made Anna's breakfast mush and bottle, then took her to comfort him and show him life was just the same.

Except as she reached out, she said her first complete sentence – well, two actually because the cat had followed her upstairs.

"I wuv you Daddy," which made him smile and cuddle her, and "My cat's called Puddy," which made him laugh out loud.

I thought perhaps she meant Pussy but she didn't. The cat was Puddy from that moment on.

Chapter Eleven

Only Molly Knows

We went on as normal – what else was there to do?

Rob was stiff with me for a few days but eventually had to relent. He wasn't petulant by nature. He needed to smile again.

Over a period of time, I explained how forward her development was, and about the incident at the house at Santa Barbara, where dead plants came back to life at her touch.

A few years passed during which time I watched Anna and her abilities grow. I tried to gently introduce Rob to her ways but he stood back suspiciously and watched as the dead leaf hanging from a house plant was returned to life.

She regarded it closely for a moment or two as if trying to get its measure, then turned it over and with great tenderness stroked its shrunken veins. Before our eyes the dull green leaf became plump and vibrant again.

There was one overriding problem on which he had to take my word.

"How are we going to send her to school? She's such empathy she'll heal everything in sight. It'll only take a kid scuffing his knees in the playground and her cover will be blown," I worried.

He was beginning to see enough of the improbable to understand in Anna's hands it sometimes became actual.

"She'll have to be schooled at home. By us to start with. If we can manage the magic and schooling together until she's older, she might have more control."

"We can't lock her up! She won't have friends to play with – she'll only have us."

"I was lucky. Uncle Joe and Dad thought I was a joke my Mum had made up, but I was nothing like Anna. All I could do was speak to dead relatives. What if Anna grew from reviving leaves to people? Oh God…the fallout could be monumental."

"*We* won't know what to do. If you think this is so serious, you have to try again to find Molly – or any of them.

"Go back to Scarsdale, but leave Anna behind this time - she and the cat can stay with me. The guys will just have to run the shop until you get back. I'll go now and organize it."

Puddy, who had grown sleek and sinuous, jumped on Anna's knee and licked her cheek.

I rang my Mum to explain. She understood the situation immediately and insisted I get there as soon as possible.

Anna and I had never been separated before, so in the meantime, I'd to try and explain to my daughter why Momma was disappearing for a while. When she got distressed, the cat bared its teeth at me and hissed. Anna dried her tears and patted its head.

"It'll be fine Pud – Momma'll be back; Mol told me so."

I was aghast. This was the first time she'd mentioned her ancestor.

Grandad Josh had said the Graham Circle was ended and a new one was to begin. Anna wasn't a Graham she was an O'Connor. Perhaps that's what he meant, or perhaps it was part of the remit of a Coven witch to pop up in whatever form wherever they chose. It was all so confusing.

The rules for home schooling in California are drastic. Your home must be registered as an educational establishment and you must prove yourself equal to the task of teaching the full curriculum. Otherwise, a qualified teacher must be engaged. I envisaged a whole string of qualified teachers at our door, leaving one after the other, after scratching themselves on a pencil sharpener or being set upon by an irate Puddy.

Rob seemed to think he could manage. Time was short. We'd twelve months to organize her schooling, so I zipped off to England and Rob went to bully the Education Authorities in LA.

Practically the first thing my Mum said to me, confirmed my private worries.

"It's possible <u>Molly</u> won't come," she said, "You knew even before you left how unreliable she was. She came to see Anna but she might decide she's done her bit now."

I burst into tears.

"She'd damn-well better come, or I'll tear that Veil to bits getting my hands round her throat."

That wouldn't work on a number of levels but it was a relief to say it.

I'd come to terms reluctantly with losing <u>Claire</u> and <u>Grandads Robert</u> and <u>Josh</u> but I'd somehow never quite let go of <u>Molly</u>.

I went to the Sisters to see if she was there.

I waited until the sun faded behind the darkening fells, and the rising wind pulling at my hair turned bitter, but still she didn't come. I was on my own to protect my child against who knew what, with the help of a husband who only half believed there was any danger at all.

"Go home NOW whispered a voice in my head, "and hide that child away. She can't control her magic — she's a danger to those around her.

"She's an Empath and Resurrectionist," continued the voice "There hasn't been one for thousands of years."

"A Resurrectionist? You mean like Burke and Hare?" I said aloud, "She's going to steal bodies?"

I knew that was ridiculous. How could a sweet little girl with her Daddy's curls and deep brown eyes dig up corpses, never mind move them.

"Fool," answered the voice. "Get on home or you'll be sorry."

The voice stopped, and as I turned to go, a last little whisper, almost inaudible, said.

"Has she found her cat yet?"

Chapter Twelve

A Shudder of Unease

When I asked my mother what she knew of witches and cats, I didn't mention Empaths and Resurrectionists.

A Wicca cat, my mother explained patiently, increased its owner's protection a hundred-fold.

Wicca cats, she said, had powers of their own, peculiar to their kind. Their chief strength was deflection – both mental and physical – and they were only ever attached to specific Coven witches. It would die for her.

This bit of information had come to her from <u>Molly</u> via <u>Claire</u> long before I was born. It had stuck in Mum's mind because of a nursery rhyme she'd learned as a child, about a cat chasing a mouse to protect a Queen. She'd always thought the cat must have loved the Queen very much, seeing as cats were so lazy and slept all day.

I explained about Puddy, and when I said the cat's name, Mum started laughing.

"The 'tort I taw' kind off the TV, or a 'pussy cat'?"

"No," I said to the last, "Not baby-talk for pussy. Its name's Puddy. Anna's quite insistent."

"Get off home, Angela. That child and Robin need you," said Mum.

I was so grateful for her understanding. I sometimes felt very alone, secreted in that corner of my mind with 'Witch' written over the door. She was the only person left alive who had experienced my abilities. At least, she was one of two, but Anna was as yet a liability rather than an asset.

I'd spoken to Rob a time or two on the phone during my stay. On the day before I left, his conversation was taut with worry.

He wasn't sure, but Rob thought Anna may have dragged Puddy out of the road again when the cat ran out of the garden. Anna appeared to have stalled a car. The bemused driver said she'd stuck out her arm in a stop gesture and the engine just died. Rob had no idea how she'd got out of the house. It sounded all too familiar.

Things appeared to be moving ahead with arranging Anna's schooling though.

Rob had been given a long list of requirements for subject teaching, which he'd had to admit we couldn't do. Neither of us were science orientated. As far as math was concerned, we could both tot up columns of figures but that was about it.

Teacher it was then. It was going to be a nightmare.

Rob was late at the airport. By the time he got there I was tapping the top of my suitcase in irritation.

Witch Ethereal

I could see him glowering even before he left the car. His hair was mussed and there was red lipstick all down his t-shirt, and a rip in his sleeve suspiciously like claw-marks.

There was a clear story behind this:

He was late because Anna had found my lipstick and daubed herself with it. He'd tried to rub it off which was why it was smeared all over the two of them. When he'd yelled at her, the cat had clawed him.

"Daddy killed Puddy," Anna told me.

Really? I turned her away. I didn't know if 'if looks could kill' might not be more than a saying where she was concerned.

"I did not," countered Rob. "I locked her in her crate."

Anna squirmed out of my arms and stared at my suitcase which skittered down the concourse and hit a bollard. My carefully packed belongings were picked up by a brisk gust of wind and scattered across the road and into the parking lot.

She turned to Robbie and screwed up her eyes.

"Better Momma's panties than you!"

She couldn't do that! I was furious. When Molly had warned me to watch her because she might be dangerous, despite her mention of Robin falling downstairs, I hadn't really believed her.

Anna knew she'd overstepped the mark.

She stood four-square in front of Rob and said:

"I'm sorry Daddy. That was bad. I love you and taking Momma's stick was stealing. I won't do it again."

I don't think Rob truly appreciated the danger he'd been in because he said:

"Words are cheap, Honey. Go and help Momma pick up her things while I turn the car round. Don't do that again – it was naughty."

"You put Puddy in jail. Don't do *that* again."

I wondered if it had sunk in what she'd done was impossible.

I took her hand before he lost his temper and she and I picked up my belongings and repacked them. This was a new thing for Robbie. He'd always been so easy-going, always the one to smooth troubled waters. His lack of knowledge was making him unsympathetic.

"Come on, Anna. You need a bath. Let's go," I said to her.

She tipped back her head and said seriously:

"I lost my temper and that was very wrong. Bad things happen when I get cross. Badder than anyone else. I try not to let them happen, but sometimes they just do. I promise I'll try harder…and I'll tell Puddy to try too."

Aside from the grammar she sounded like an adult.

"I know, Sweetheart. But you and I are going to have to sit down and have a serious talk. There are things you need to understand."

Witch Ethereal

"The witch thing? I know – <u>Molly</u> told me."

Chapter Thirteen

Explanations and Empathy

After we'd got home and I'd played with Anna while she bathed, then put her to bed, and a newly released and miffed Puddy curled up next to her cheek, I looked down at our daughter.

Anna had long eyelashes like her Dad, long enough to throw tiny shadows under her eyes as they fluttered shut. She'd my pink and white complexion, and I noticed with a jolt, her mouth was an exact replica of Molly's – same bowed top and plump bottom lips, soft and slightly open as she slept. But her most telling feature was the waterfall of chestnut curls, just like Robbie's, which presently fell across her cheek and over the cat.

Anna was quite lovely – soft, beautiful…...and deadly.

Rob walked up behind me, and putting his arms round my waist, propped his chin on my shoulder.

"I don't understand what to do for the best…how to help her – how to help you."

"You're not alone. I don't know either. I suppose it's to our advantage she loves us and means us no harm, but then she's not always in control of her actions. All three of us are going to have to learn fresh lessons."

Poor Rob was all at sea so, in an effort to lighten his mood, I continued:

Witch Ethereal

"I never thought I'd ever say this, but it's a relief your mother's not here. She might have been unintentionally holidaying in Hawaii."

The very thought sent him off into fits of laughter. I was glad of it – he'd been so worried. If he could come to understand our nature, it would be easier for him to deal with.

Anna gave a gentle snore as she turned in her sleep, and her arm draped protectively over her beloved pet.

The following morning early, Rob had an appointment with a new client, so he was up, smartly dressed and out of the door before Anna was ready to face the day.

It wouldn't have been wise to delay our conversation, so after breakfast, I laid Anna's box of pencils and sketch pad on the kitchen counter-top and waited for her to settle. Like me, she was always calmed by drawing.

"You remember me saying we needed to have a little talk?"

"Uh-huh," she said concentrating on her picture.

"Listen to me Anna because this is very important. Mostly it's about Daddy but there are other things too."

She obediently placed her pencil back in its box and gave me her undivided attention.

"I know you sometimes speak to <u>Molly</u>. Do you see her?"

"No. She's in my head."

"Molly is Grandma's grandma in England. She is the best witch I ever knew – a Coven witch. I'll explain that later – for now you need to understand they are the most powerful kind. When you were just a few weeks old, I took you to meet Molly and she told me all about you.

"Molly can travel across the Veil and talk to people on both sides. She used to play catch with me when I was small. The Veil is…"

"She told me all about the Veil."

"That's good. All witches can cross the Veil at certain times, but Molly comes and goes as she wishes.

"I'm a witch too. In England, I could see and speak to dead people – but only those I had a blood link with, although there was one big exception, my Auntie Claire. More of that later, too."

"Molly believes that you are the most gifted witch she ever knew. She calls you an Empath, which means you read people's thoughts and look for the good there. Also, you are a Resurrectionist which is a bit more difficult to explain.

"You haven't learned yet how to do it properly, but you can give back life when it's gone – like you can with the leaves on Momma's plants."

I knew she'd understood me on the deepest level when she said:

"That's plants. Can I do it with creatures too? Creatures like Puddy or even the little wren that built her nest in the camelia near the pool? Puddy killed her last summer. I was very cross with her – it had the sweetest song. I would have tried to give her back her life if I'd known."

I hadn't known about the bird.

"I don't know, Honey. Perhaps. When you're bigger, perhaps."

"And people? Will I be able to give back life to people?"

What did I say to that?

"I don't know and neither did Molly. We'll just have to wait and see."

She looked at me thoughtfully for a moment or two, then with no rancor said:

"You don't know much, do you Momma? How can you help me if you don't know anything?"

Oh Lord!

"We'll just have to learn together. Molly said the last witch with your powers lived thousands of years ago."

She looked inordinately pleased, and I'd to remind myself ordinary children liked to be told they had something special too.

"Is that all, Mom? Can I go play now?" Anna asked, hopefully.

"Not just yet. There's the most important thing of all."

"Can I get a juice then? I'm thirsty," she said, her attention wandering.

At my nod, she jumped down off her stool, took a beaker from the cupboard and filled it from a bottle in the fridge. This was a new thing she'd started doing, and she was still finding it difficult to lift the bottle. Nine times out of ten, some of the juice ended up on the floor. She always told Puddy to lick it up, which she did with relish.

Anna took a good slurp, slid the beaker carefully onto the countertop and climbed back on her stool, looking at me seriously.

"You can go on now," she said.

Hmm…

"The rest, for now, concerns Daddy. Daddy isn't a witch…"

She guffawed loudly.

"Of course not. He's a guy. Everyone knows guys aren't witches."

"I don't think most people know about witches at all, Anna."

She seemed genuinely surprised.

"Not being a witch means Daddy can't look after himself around our kind. Sometimes, I think without knowing it, you take advantage of that. Like you did when you threw down my suitcase at the airport. Things like that scare Dad and he doesn't know what to do. It's up to you to look after him. You're an Empath. You know he loves you more than anything in the world."

She nodded.

"More even than you…....which is saying something."

I hadn't known that. Perhaps I'd been neglecting him recently.

"I need your help too, Darling. I'd be vulnerable faced with a witch like Molly even."

"What's vun…vuera…vunerable?" she asked with some difficulty. I thanked the Lord there were some things I knew she didn't. For the moment at least. "It means I may not be clever enough to protect myself.

"Part of being a witch is knowing when to speak and when to keep quiet especially around strangers. Most people – even women – are like Daddy. They don't understand and may try to harm you because you're different.

"Not Dad," I added hastily, "I need you to look out for Dad in secret, and never lose your temper when he's around. Think you can do that?"

She looked as if she'd been given a military command.

"I will do that Momma. I WILL. Don't worry. I'll keep him safe. And I won't let Puddy scratch him either – well, I'll try."

"Daddy knows I'm a witch – you too – but he can't bring himself to really believe it, even when it happens in front of him, like at the airport. He thinks you're like me – my powers are just seeing dead relatives. That's pretty harmless and I can easily hide it. You can do much more. Molly has warned us to be very careful."

"Yes," Anna said thoughtfully, chewing the end of a pencil, "She told me too."

It should have been more difficult explaining to her why she couldn't go to school like the other kids. Rob took this one:

"Kids called Stan don't do school."

Strangely enough, she accepted that as read. Perhaps it was part of the 'looking after dad' deal.

The first day of 'school' began. We'd bought her a little desk and chair and put it in the conservatory where there were few distractions.

I could have cried.

There sat this little mite, all alone in a small navy uniform we'd devised, with Anna embroidered in yellow on her shirt collar. Before her were a brand-new set of sharpened pencils, a notebook, and an eraser. She looked at me expectantly, waiting for me to say something teacher-ish.

"Wow, Stan!" exclaimed her Dad. "Don't you look the bee's knees? You'll be in Wellesley before you're twelve."

"What's Wellesley?"

"It's where all the posh rich kids go. The ones with millionaires for Dads."

He looked at her with satisfaction and winked.

"Like you."

Anna rolled her eyes and tutted. She couldn't imagine anyone less posh than her silly Dad."

At that point the table and chair were consigned to the attic, and Anna started on her ABCs sitting on her Daddy's knee, while he pulled faces when she got it wrong and made her giggle.

Chapter Fourteen
Anna, Rob and an Education

The teacher arrived. The first one, that is.

We'd been given a list of names with their owners' specialist subjects. We could manage the English and art side of things, so we picked out a young girl called Carol Lustig who specialized in math with some sciences.

She was fresh out of college and turned up neat and smart carrying a hold-all of lesson plans which Anna eyed with trepidation.

"Good morning, Mrs. O'Connor," Carol said politely, "and to you Miss O'Connor."

She bent down so her face was level with my daughter's. Puddy spat at her and she withdrew quickly. Anna pushed the cat away.

"Good morning, Miss Lustig. I'm happy to make your acquaintance."

I judged from Miss Lustig's expression that this was a bit of a surprise from a five-year-old. We knew she was forward for her age, but never saw her from any other perspective than our own. That she could discuss the physiology of cats just meant she was interested in Puddy to me. Rob, whose life was based outside our home, sometimes remarked on it.

Miss Lustig lasted longer than her later colleagues simply by virtue of her ability to ignore the impossible, but by Anna's seventh birthday it was decided she'd taught her everything she knew, and we should find a middle school teacher. She was good enough to stay on until she was replaced by Mrs. Johnstone, who lasted as long as could be expected after seeing Anna fix plants and revive a dead fly on the windowsill.

We decided to try a man next, thinking perhaps he might be less intimidated by a small girl with shining curls and dimples. Mr. Rossi, a handsome Italian-American, was sacked after a month, when Anna told us he 'sold poisonous medicine to sick people'. Rob detected immediately he was involved in the drug trade, which Anna confirmed.

So, what now? It was clear Anna, unwittingly, would dispose of every teacher presented to her.

There appeared to be no other course but to lie to the authorities and hope we could take up enough of the slack to put her through her first set of external examinations ourselves.

Of course, Anna picked up on how concerned we were, especially her much-loved Dad who was completely perplexed by matters he couldn't hope to understand. She truly did redouble her efforts after Mr. Ricci. Perhaps that's why slowly she began to conqueror her gifts and to gain control much earlier than I'd expected. I don't know if completing her school exams early with full marks was magic or just hard work, but she did that too."

One day over breakfast, as Anna was playing on the lawn with Puddy, I said to Robbie:

"You are so unhappy, Darling. I want to see you smile again. Do you realize how little you do that these days? Your smile was the sexiest thing about you. It's what I fell in love with."

He looked even unhappier if that were possible.

"Don't you love me anymore then? I knew sooner or later I'd lose you. I'm Robin O'Connor of Ghyll Howe farm, son of Irish immigrants Dermot and Deidra O'Connor – you're Angela Greenwood of Scarsdale Manor Farm whose father and uncle own a great chunk of Westmoreland."

I lost my temper.

"You idiot! I'm Angela O'Connor, wife of Robin O'Connor – what was it once you dubbed yourself? – 'Photographer to the Stars'. Well, you might not have been then but you certainly are now. And as for the 'owning' bit, you're a multi-millionaire businessman. Don't be such an idiot."

His eyes brimmed with tears but he didn't speak.

It was then I saw a small movement out of the corner of my eye. We both turned to see Anna with Puddy at her feet, standing motionless in the doorway.

She regarded us for a moment or two before saying:

"If we can't explain it, Momma, we're just going to have to show him. We're making him unhappy."

Rob ran to her and picked her up, cuddling her tight to his chest. She pushed herself away and looked him square in the eye.

"Mom can't show you. She left everything behind in England so she could be with you. She loves you Daddy and so do I."

He cried into her shoulder.

"If you love us you will just have to be brave while I show you things. I know I promised you Momma, but you know this must be done."

I'd never seen her look nervous before. She was testing the strength of the connection between us. What if it broke? What if he just couldn't take it? We had to learn if Kilimanjaro was a belief as well as a diamond ring.

But this was much more. This was a test of her perfect control for the first time. She had always been able to begin – now we had to find out if she could stop.

It turned out Anna was her father's daughter through and through. A true empath, she made him laugh.

Very slowly, a disgruntled Puddy rose, still sitting, two or three feet into the air. The cat didn't seem able to move a muscle but the disgust on its face was unmistakable.

Anna brought it gently back to the floor and released it. It shot out of the door and hid amongst the rose bushes at the edge of the pool. Anna shrugged.

"She'll get over it."

"How did you do that?" laughed my husband. "You really trained Pud well."

Anna stamped her foot in irritation.

"Nothing else for it Momma. I only learned this yesterday so just pray it works or a little creature will suffer."

"Please forgive me for what I'm going to do Dad, but you must understand. You must, or we can't be a family."

I was filled with trepidation. I had no idea where this was going and it didn't exactly fill me with confidence that Rob was gazing at her lovingly with a smile on his face.

"Go on, Sweetheart. Sounds exciting."

I buried my head in my hands. Was my life about to end?

We had a birdfeeder hanging from a tree in the garden. Anna spent hours watching the birds flit to and fro and listening to their songs.

A tiny goldfinch, its feathers resplendent, sat on the feeder's apex. Enchanted by its beauty we stopped to watch as it opened its beak and filled the air with its joy of living.

I saw Anna's hand move sharply sideways, half-hidden by the folds of her skirt.

The bird stopped in mid-song and dropped like a stone to lie unmoving on the grass, its tiny claws clenched as if it still clung to its perch.

If I was horrified, Rob looked as if he was about to cross the Veil. The color had left his face and he stared, open-mouthed between his daughter and the dead bird lying feet up at the base of the feeder.

"Don't worry, Dad," said Anna when he began hyperventilating, "I can fix it. But first you have to believe it's true."

She took his hand and sleep-walked him across the lawn.

"Pick it up," she encouraged.

Robbie did as she said. The goldfinch lay soft and warm on his palm, eyes closed and bill still ajar from its song.

Anna began to sing an ordinary little lullaby – Golden Slumbers, I think it was – and gently stroked its chest over and over.

Nothing happened. She started to look worried. Her mouth set and she concentrated harder.

"I'm new at this. I need to think more."

In the blink of an eye, the tiny creature flicked over on Robbie's palm, then darted off between the trees into the blue sky. It was the most amazing thing I ever saw.

"Wow Stan, where'd you learn hypnosis?" said the only man on earth stupider than my Dad.

Anna sat on the ground in disbelief.

"What do I do now Mom?"

"There's none so blind as those who just will not see," I said, glaring at her Dad. "Nothing you can do."

Chapter Fifteen

Anna Meets Katy and Lena

If it proved nothing else, the incident with the bird showed me I could trust Anna's control of her gifts. I told her to tell <u>Molly</u> what had happened and ask her advice.

Meanwhile, I decided it was time to cut Rob some slack, and between us, Anna and I formed a plan, where I would get the odd day off and she could spend time alone with her Dad. I didn't need to tell her; she instinctively understood to keep her magic in check. I hoped she would use her empathy to comfort him.

In return, Rob could have time to himself, and I would take over. Neither Anna nor I believed she should yet be left alone but I was sure it wouldn't be long.

It had been three excruciatingly long years, and she still had no friends. As soon as possible, that had to be fixed. By the time she was nine, we figured she was ready to be let loose on the world. It helped that she was empathetic so felt when people were unhappy with her. I just prayed her temper wouldn't override her good sense.

With time to myself I began to meet up with Cam again. It was so good to get out of the house and a relief to drink wine with my friend and to see the people I'd met through her.

Of course, the topics of conversation had changed. No longer were husbands' new cars or trips to Europe at the top of the agenda. It had been over four years, and some now had children of their own...including Cam and Nik.

They were the proud parents of an eight-year-old daughter called Catherine who Cam had brought along to one of our lunches. Known to one and all as Katy, she was shy, demur and answered questions with a single word.

Katy was a pretty girl, in the way of mixed-race children. She had a perfect bronze skin and spectacular, almond-shaped green eyes. She would surpass her mother's beauty as she grew.

There were one or two other children there, but as I was only very briefly acquainted with their mothers, I didn't exchange more than a word or two with either.

I learned from Cam that Nik was concluding a business deal in Marrakech, of all places. Rob, I told her, was still deeply immersed in his love of photography.

She sat Katy on her knee.

"This is my friend Angela," smiled Cam.

Katy shrank into her arms from where she eyed me nervously.

"I don't bite," I smiled, kindly. "I have a little girl too. She's a bit older than you and her name's Anastasia –

we call her Anna for short, because her grandmother says it's too long to call her in when she's outside playing."

I began to tell Katy about Anna and how she had a cat with a funny name and loved birds and dolls except Barbie which she hated.

She began hesitantly to unwind and gave me a tentative smile.

"Perhaps I could bring her to meet you?" I asked in a speaking-to-children tone, "Would you like that?"

Cam was pleased.

"She's so shy. I would like her to have more friends but she finds it difficult. With Nik out at work and me off on tour she spends a lot of time with a nanny, which doesn't help. They only seem to go to the park or the beach so she spends her time with adults."

She looked surprised when Katy said:

"Can I Maman? Can I see Anna?"

"Tell you what," I said, "Why don't the four of us meet up for lunch somewhere where the kiddies can play uninterrupted and we can drink wine in the same way."

"Oh good!" said Katy, suddenly animated, "Can we go to a drive-in Maman and eat burgers and drink soda? Can we please?"

She stopped to think, uncertain.

"Do you think Anna would like that?" she asked.

Her face fell.

"I won't mind if she doesn't."

"Like it? I think she'd be over the moon. She's never been to a drive-in either. Perhaps she could bring Puddy. On second thoughts, that might not be such a good idea."

I smiled inwardly at the thought of the havoc Anna and Puddy together could have wreaked in a drive-in when she was younger.

It couldn't have gone better. The two little girls, although shy at first, got on like a house on fire.

We went to see some silly cartoons at the drive-in, but as Cam disapproved strongly of soda and burgers, we sat on the beach instead and ate ice cream.

Cam and I relaxed in the sunshine while the little ones stripped down to their panties and splashed about in the gentle waves at the sea's edge.

When we decided it was time to leave, Cam went to dispose of our lunch wrappings and I ran down with a towel to dry off the girls and bring them back to the car.

As I turned, one child at each hand and the towel thrown over my shoulder, I saw Cam talking to another woman with a couple of small children, a boy and a girl.

It wasn't until I drew closer I recognized Lena. I'd only met her once before but vividly remembered the feeling of unease. It was nothing to the girls' reaction though.

Lena's children stared at them blankly, and Katy began to back away, but Anna was staring at their mother and

I watched a darkness I'd never seen before cloud her eyes. She'd stiffened, then turning, took Katy by the hand and walked her down the beach, where they sat staring from behind an empty lounger.

It would have been impolite to avoid Lena after she'd seen me. She shook my hand again and I felt the same coldness, even though she was smiling at me.

"This is Sandy and the little one is Marcus. Say hello, children."

I would say they matched our children in age, with Sandy being the older. They said hello in unison and I got the impression they did everything together.

"Hi, kids," said Cam, smiling. "Why don't you go and find our girls and play for a while?"

They ran dutifully off but I saw with alarm Anna and Katy weren't where I'd last seen them. In fact, I couldn't see them at all. When Sandy and Marcus came back alone, I began to really worry.

Just as I was about to excuse myself and go in search of them, there was a loud shout and a stout man in swim shorts dashed down the beach, spittle flying, eyes and mouth wide with horror. Twenty yards behind him stood our two little girls hand in hand. I thanked God no-one else knew my daughter's story.

"What on earth was that about do you think?" said Cam, curiously. "Thank goodness the kids were well away from him. He looked crazy."

Things happened between both sets of children. No-one else would have noticed, but I was aware of these things. Katy looked up at Anna for reassurance and Anna squeezed her hand, looking straight at me. Lena's kids grinned at each other.

They said their goodbyes, and as I was about to shake Lena's hand, Anna reached up and took mine instead. Lena was friendly enough but cast a perplexed glance at Anna before walking away.

"Well," said Cam, as we walked back to the car, "wonder what happened there?"

Chapter Sixteen
Alone Time

We dropped Cam and Katy off and went home. Anna had grasped all I wanted to know, of that I was certain.

I stood her in the bath to rinse away the sand and salt, and as I washed her hair, I said:

"Come on – spill. I think you owe me a few explanations, don't you?"

Anna wiped shampoo away from her eyes and looked at me long and hard.

"It had to be done," she said, "whether you like it or not."

It suddenly came to me we were growing apart. Anna was an eight-year-old adult – not only that, but an adult who could plaster me across the ceiling if she wanted to. I'd been wrong assessing her skills. She talked to Molly but couldn't see her, but she could move things around even with her back turned, as well as restoring life. I hoped that was all.

"What had to be done?" I asked, nervously.

"Well, first…Katy is afraid of those children – the girl took her to the restroom once when all the Mom's were together and slapped her…hard. Katy isn't strong like me – I'd have hit Sandy back – or worse.

"Her mother's Wicca. Don't go near her, her gift is ill-wishing – she's a hostile. She's not very strong because she needs to touch. Don't ever touch her – she's not a good person and neither is her daughter. The little boy doesn't matter," she added dismissively.

"And……"

"Katy was afraid so I took her further down the beach where she couldn't be seen. Then this man came up to us and started touching my hair and stroking Katy's cheek. He was awful, Mom. I hit him over the head with his beach umbrella. Don't worry, nobody saw."

"I take it the umbrella flew through the air first."

"Of course it did, I'm only eight, I couldn't possibly have lifted it."

"You know if Katy says anything we're going to have a problem explaining this to her Mom, don't you? Then she'll discuss it with your Daddy and we'll both be in trouble."

"Katy won't say anything. I told her not to. She's my friend now, so she'll do as I say. I'll go to bed early if you like so you can explain it to Daddy."

She was capable of great harm. It was enough to worry <u>Molly</u> who was known for not caring much about anything.

The front door banged.

"Hello, my beautiful girls. Come and kiss Daddy, lots – you too Angie."

"I'll go now, then, shall I?" said, Anna raising an eyebrow.

"Kiss him first – and mean it."

"I always mean it with Daddy – I love him to the moon and back," said my daughter in one of her eight-year-old moods.

Rob tucked 'Stan' into bed and read her about Hansel and Gretel. The book before had been 'Narnia' and had a snow queen who was a wicked witch. Anna, naturally, thought it was rubbish but she never told her Dad so.

When he came back, all smiley from cuddling his daughter, he said:

"I'm glad all this silliness has gone away and she's just a normal little girl again."

We ate pasta together. As he half-drowned his in grated cheese, I said:

"About that. We need to talk……"

"Not now, Angela," he said sharply, "Another time."

Robbie was usually pretty good at gaging my mood, but not this time. Even Anna knew this was important. I needed to find a way to get him in the mood to listen and there was only one way to do that – his camera, believe it or not. When he was concentrating on his shots every other consideration melted away.

"Rob, I'd like some photos of you and me for that gap on the dining room wall. Maybe you could do some of Anna in the morning too. We don't have any good family shots."

"Great idea – I've got my Nikon in the car. I'll go get it. Make a nice change from weird blokes with tatts. Go and tart yourself up a bit."

I sat before my dressing table mirror. It was true an afternoon on the beach had left me the worse for wear. My long hair was knotted from the breeze but my skin, make-up free, was glowing.

I'd been untangling my hair strand by strand for some time before I noticed Rob had been photographing me. He was so good at that – his subject was rarely aware of his presence.

"These are going to be completely brilliant. You're a beautiful woman. I'm unbelievably lucky – married to such a doll. Let's make love – maybe there'll be a boy this time! I'd forgotten about the football team. I need some action."

The thoughts became more disjointed as his breathing deepened and his eyes became hooded. He was losing it big-time.

Rob wrestled me to the ground. Whilst my brain was still functioning – which it wasn't for long – it occurred to me he wasn't usually this passionate. He enjoyed the foreplay as much as sex itself, but in this instance seemed almost desperate and…... it was at that point I no longer cared.

Afterwards, we lay on the floor completely spent. Our legs were still intertwined and as I moved to snuggle into his arms my attention was directed to two, small bare feet level with my face.

My eyes travelled upwards in increasing horror to see our daughter gazing down at us as we lay, sweaty and panting on the floor.

Puddy was snuggled in her arms, and her expression noncommittal. After a few seconds of total silence, she said:

"You'd better tell her Daddy. It'll be worse if you don't."

She walked out of the door.

Chapter Seventeen.

A Cataclysmic Shock for Angela

"What…what do you have to tell me?" I asked with apprehension. "What does she mean? Did you do something I should know about?"

"No, of course not," he said zipping up his pants and fastening the buckle on his belt. "I've no idea what she's talking about."

I'd have believed him had he been able to look me in the eye.

For the first time in an age, Rob was unusually attentive.

At Anna's insistence, we walked along the street to a small bar we used to go to when we first moved into Reina del Sur, when our marriage was fresh and there were just the two of us.

Before we left, Rob took my engagement ring from the jewelry box on my dresser and slid it onto my finger, kissing my hand then my lips as he did so.

Our estrangement had come on so gradually it was only at that moment I realized we had completely lost touch. We never talked any more. I'd no idea about his work – he used to enthuse about it all the time – to tell me who his new clients were, about the people who worked for him and those he met every day. My life was taken up with Anna but there was so much I couldn't tell him I ended up saying nothing at all.

Now, in the evenings we ate together, and made small talk before he went to work in his home studio. We went to bed – sometimes we made love, sometimes we didn't. There was a time passion overcame common sense. No more.

Anna was right. We did need to talk. Although she clearly thought there was something in particular we should say.

I was notoriously dim at this kind of thing.

Back at Scarsdale Grandad Greenwood told me my people were annoyed with me because I was hurting them through my own pain. He'd said he couldn't tell me why, but if I looked in my heart I would know.

The answer to the conundrum turned out to be Rob, and it was true I knew it but wouldn't admit we were destined to be together even to myself. Now I was pushing him away again and things were beginning to turn sour.

We were both at fault, but only I had the key to fix it, that was if I could find it.

When I was sick and tired of mulling it over, I decided to take Anna to see the dinosaurs at the Natural History Museum in LA.

We spent a pleasant hour in there, then when my feet began to ache, Anna very considerately suggested we eat ice cream. There was a parlor in the next street, but I proposed we drive a couple of miles up the road where there was a spectacular place Rob had once taken me to.

As I told her about it, she nodded her head vigorously, but then tossed her long curls, and took my hand as we walked to the parking lot. All the way there she was silent, apparently fascinated by the garden on her side of the path.

I tried to initiate conversation on the car journey, but she seemed preoccupied, so eventually I said:

"You're very quiet, Darling. Is something wrong?"

She was silent for so long I wondered if she was going to speak at all.

"Not yet," she said. "Look Momma, I just don't feel like chatting right now. Must be all those dead dinosaurs we saw at the museum."

She stuck out her bottom lip and stared straight forward.

Sometimes her behavior was unfathomable and I had to remind myself she saw and heard much more than most people. No doubt she'd tell me in her own good time.

The ice cream parlor was part of a complex of other eateries about twenty minutes' drive from the museum. In order to get there from the parking lot, we'd to walk past the front of a burger joint and a pleasant bistro with a shade and tables outside.

As we drew level with the bistro, Anna paused to tie the laces on her trainers which had become loose, and I stopped to wait for her, taking her hand as she stood.

It was the first time she'd looked at me since we'd left the museum, and I was surprised how angry and strained she appeared.

Unexpectedly, there was a loud crash as a waiter's tray hit the paving between the tables, and its contents smashed and skittered across the ground. Everyone turned to look, and those closest stood to dust down their clothes, now covered in debris.

It was then I saw my husband. He'd risen from his seat and was helping a young woman sitting at his table to her feet. She had a slight glass cut on one cheek which was seeping blood.

"Look, there's Daddy. Isn't that a lovely surprise? Let's go say hello."

We were standing at their table before I realized that my Robbie still had hold of Layla's hand.

LAYLA! Zella's housemate before she left California.

I hadn't seen her since Joe's wedding. Zella had been surprised when she suddenly stopped returning her calls.

Then I remembered Robin squiring her around Nethershaw like some Victorian heartbreaker and raving about the photo he'd taken of her on the fells. I'd believed he was trying to make me jealous.

I froze in horror – so did he.

Witch Ethereal

Our daughter let go of my hand.

"I told you, Daddy," she said, as she skipped past him and introduced herself to Layla.

"How do you do. I'm Anna O'Connor. This is my Momma, Angela – but of course you know each other, don't you? My Daddy you've run into already."

Anna smiled winningly. It reminded me of <u>Deidra</u>, Robin's mother – a hand grenade with the pin pulled. Rob had clearly had the same thought. He took Layla by the arm and left.

So……what now?

Chapter Eighteen

The End of the Beginning

I stood outside a fashionable little bistro in one of the better suburbs of Los Angeles, surrounded by broken glass, splashed with wine, smeared with cream and frozen rigid with shock.

I don't know how long I stood there, or even where I was. The only thing I recognized was Robbie's gentle brown eyes in the face of his daughter.

She picked up my purse, took my arm and as gently as a mother with a newborn baby, led me back to my car where she sat beside me until I came to myself again. In a quiet voice she said.

"I wasn't allowed to tell, or I would have. The only thing I could do, I did. I warned Daddy to tell the truth before it was too late. But I don't think it's too late yet…not yet.

"Why didn't you tell me what was happening?"

"I just told you – I wasn't allowed to."

"Allowed? What do you mean 'allowed'? If you knew Daddy was doing this, you should have told me so I could try to fix it. How did you know what was going on?

She remained silent, then:

"Not now…later, when you're not so upset. Let's go home."

Witch Ethereal

There didn't seem anything else left to do. I didn't know where Rob was. I didn't even know if I wanted to know. The only thing left to do was to go home.

I tried to pour myself a glass of red wine, but my hands were shaking so much I spilled it over our white suite.

I filled the glass again, drank it then drank another. Anna poured the rest of the bottle down the sink.

"What bloody good will that do?" she scolded.

She was eight and already we'd driven her to bad language.

"You'll get mad next, Momma. We should go somewhere where you can break things that won't matter."

After I'd pelted the French windows with eggs and tipped half a barrowful of compost into the pool, I was so worn out, if Rob had walked through the door, I'd have been too exhausted to do anything about it so I cried instead.

A week went by......then a month. Still no Rob.

If I'd had the wit to realize it at the time, it was only a rerun of his disappearing act before we were married. He'd made himself a millionaire to prove his worth, not only to me, but to the whole world.

But I didn't – have the wit, that is.

When it got to six weeks and he'd still to show, I packed a bag for Anna and me, gave cat food to the lady next door so Puddy wouldn't starve, locked the house, and without a backward glance went back to England. Rather than being alone, I may as well be with people who loved me.

My husband had shown his metal big time. I'd always known he was a fly-by-night but I thought he'd changed - he'd tried so hard to win me. Well, apparently I was wrong.

I'd told no-one I was coming so expected a shouting at from my mother and a tearful greeting from Dad but it didn't happen.

There was a natural order to things and Anna came first. She was hugged and kissed until she could take no more. Then it was my turn.

"He's at the Sisters," said my mother, unasked.

For a moment I was speechless.

"What's he doing *there*?"

"He's been staying at Ghyll Howe with Sean and Rona. We didn't know he was here until he brought his bike out for a run this morning."

"Anna and I will go to Smyltandale then. You can tell him I won't see him. I don't suppose he's told you why we're here? How long has he been here anyway?"

"He told us his problems in glorious Technicolor, and he's been here…" began my mother, but she was pulled up short when Anna said:

"Four and a half weeks."

Witch Ethereal

We stared at her.

"How on earth did you know that, Sweetheart?" said my mother. "You're exactly right. Today is the…" she checked the calendar tacked to the side of the dresser, "Today's the thirteenth and he told me he'd arrived at Ghyll Howe on the seventeenth of last month."

"I don't suppose it occurred to you to pick up the phone? We've been waiting in a state of panic for the whole of that time."

"*You* have," said Anna, "I kept telling you it was still okay."

"Bit difficult to let you know when we didn't know ourselves," my mother said shortly. Then her voice softened, "You must be so upset, Sweetie. The grownups in your life are behaving dreadfully. They don't deserve you."

"Oh no, Grandmother. I'm not sad. I'll leave that to those two."

My daughter skipped out of the door and went to look curiously around the yard.

There isn't much that fazes my mother but she didn't quite know what to say next, except to burst out with:

"I wish Deidra was here."

The effects of this would have been two-fold: Deidra would've talked manners to Anna until one of them fell asleep, and then she'd have called Rob a waste of space, and a woman-mad tart, not fit to be the father of such a well-mannered child.

But she wasn't there. She was gone beyond the Veil where we couldn't reach her. In that minute I missed her more than ever before and my eyes filled with tears. My mother was immediately contrite.

"Sorry Angela, that was unforgiveable," she whispered.

We ended up sobbing in each other's arms.

My Dad was already shouting to Mum as he came to the door.

"Who's the kid poking about in the yard? She was swinging on the rails looking at those two orphan lambs. Cheeky little bugger. She said 'Hi there, Grandfather' as I walked past. I didn't think I looked that old."

He'd rived off his boots on the scraper by the door before he saw me, then almost fell over his feet running to pick me up.

I never felt so unconditionally loved as when my Dad hugged me. He was the absolute opposite of Rob – totally dependable. We were both laughing and crying by turns.

"Perhaps you'd better go and greet your granddaughter," I told him.

"Anastasia…that was Anastasia? Well blow me!"

"Anna, Dad. We…I call her Anna."

Anna returned, and my Dad picked her up as if she was a toddler and jiggled her about, calling out her name and saying, 'Well I never – Anna O'Connor, as I live and breathe.'

"Is <u>Molly</u> here?" asked Anna at last, pushing him away, "I can feel her and her voice is loud."

"Tomorrow…we'll talk about it all tomorrow," said my mother hurriedly. "Meanwhile, why don't you let Mummy show you Smyltandale Cottage. Auntie Zella says it was built by fairies."

Then to me:

"Dad'll fetch your bags and there's a couple of TV dinners in the freezer down there. What do I say to Robbie?"

"Whatever you like. There's nothing he can possibly say to put things right so please yourself."

It was absolutely true Robin couldn't have done or said a single thing to make everything better – but fortunately it wasn't his opinion that counted.

The following morning, Anna and I walked the few yards from the cottage to the pack-bridge. She took off her shoes and socks and paddled about in some rockpools at the base of the moss-encrusted pilings, giggling as the minnows tickled her toes.

She had never seen anything quite like it and looked about her in delight.

"I thought you were kidding when you said it was a fairy-tale cottage. Naturally it has nothing to do with real fairies – just the ones in story books."

Weird child.

"Come on. I'll pour you a bowl of Frosties and we'll see if Grannie– don't call her Grandmother, she'll hate it – has left us some milk in the fridge."

"Then can we go and see Daddy?"

"No!" I snapped, brusquer than intended. "No, not yet."

"You do realize, Momma, you're going to have to speak to him sooner or later. You can't leave me stuck in the middle."

Rob's bike had gone by then, so really to get out of the way I borrowed Mum's car, and went to Bythwaite to cry on Zella's shoulder, leaving Anna at Scarsdale.

Unbeknown to me at the time, on the pretext of business, Dad took Anna over to Ghyll Howe with him, thinking Rob would be there, but he wasn't. Sean said they hadn't seen him for a couple of days and had thought he'd stayed at Scarsdale.

Dad and Anna were back for tea.

Another bloody disappearing act from Rob!

Unfortunately – or perhaps fortunately, depending how you looked at it - it was I who found him.

At Bythwaite. I stayed for something to eat so I could catch Joe when he came in from work. While I waited, as they were so close, I took a walk up to the Sisters. I'd only to climb uphill across a couple of fields bordering the lane opposite the farm gate.

Whatever the weather, there always seemed to be a chill to the air there, and that day I felt it especially keenly. A distant lapwing called from the other side of Gastal Crag, its contralto notes whipped away by a strengthening wind.

I shivered and pulled my cardigan tight against the cold. I hoped the Ladies would be kind. They sometimes weren't when there was conflict on our side of the Veil.

The last few yards were up a steep rise which overlooked our home at Scarsdale.

I should have been surprised to see Rob standing on the edge of the ridge and looking down across the valley to the fells beyond, hands deep in his pockets, but I wasn't. He was silhouetted against a deepening sunset.

What *did* surprise me was that Anna was holding his hand. I'd thought she was as angry as me. I should have known better, this was her adored Dad."

"See, you didn't believe me. Here she is!" Anna said, gazing up into the face of a man I hardly recognized.

Mum had described her father, my Grandad Robert Graham to me, as he was just before he died, worn out by his interrupted love for Aunt Claire, and the raising of three children in a half-ruined croft on a Westmoreland hillside.

That was how my Rob looked.

Silver marred his gorgeous chestnut curls and the lines around his mouth had deepened. The eyes which looked into mine were defensive, but devoid of emotion. I realized I must have looked much the same. It had only been six weeks – just six weeks.

He waited for me to speak but I just couldn't think of a single thing to say.

"Oh, for the love of God," groaned Anna, looking heavenwards. "Say something…if only goodbye!"

She was nine years old and she was behaving as if we were the children.

"Molly is so cross – I've passed on her message not to worry over and over, but you still think you know better."

Rob dropped her hand and stepped backwards.

"There is no Molly, Anna. If there was, I would ask for her help. I'd ask for anybody's help right now."

Oh Lord, there was Molly standing next to Anna with a face like thunder, and he'd no idea she was there. She said to me:

"Anna hears the echo of my voice but can't see me. It's her only weakness."

Anna flinched, and I was astounded to see a fleeting shadow of apprehension cross Molly's features.

"Other than that, she has just about every other gift I ever heard of."

"If I understood what that meant, I might have an opinion one way or the other," I snapped, instantly slipping back into our familiar relationship, "But I don't. Meanwhile Robin's looking at me as if I've completely lost it. I've managed to persuade him into believing in

Claire, but he still thinks you're my imaginary friend, like Dad does."

"Good day, Ma'am," said Molly and threw a kiss in Anna's direction. They smiled at each other as if sharing a joke.

"I'll go then," said Anna, "and leave you grownups to work this out between you."

The last was said with a liberal dose of sarcasm.

I was so shaken by their exchange, I sat down hard on the turf next to Molly's grave.

"What the hell's going on?" demanded Rob, as Anna disappeared down the slope, humming loudly to herself.

Molly sat on the top of one of the megaliths and watched developments with interest.

It was difficult to explain to Robin. I could see and hear her, Anna could hear her and he could do neither. I'd half convinced him with a snap he'd taken in Nethershaw churchyard where he photographed Claire's grave, and although she couldn't appear to him, she'd managed to show up in the picture. It was bad enough that I could do crazy things, but when it came to his daughter he blew a gasket.

I told him what had happened.

"Molly called her Ma'am? What the hell for?" he said, our imminent divorce put momentarily on a back burner. "She's nine years old. She's only just learned to kick a ball, for God's sake."

"Kick a ball? Not that again! She's also the most powerful witch Molly's ever known."

He guffawed.

"She's not even in High School yet!"

"You've seen her bring a bird back to life, regrow plant leaves, and yes, it was Anna who upended that waiter's tray. She wanted me to see what you were up to!"

"What I was up to? How do you know 'what I was up to'. You've never bloody asked."

"And how do you suggest I do that, genius, when you disappear without trace for six weeks?"

I had him there. He'd no answer.

Chapter Nineteen
Anna Almighty

Rob walked off and crouched, hunched, next to the biggest monolith, being careful not to touch it.

His voice was so low I'd to move closer to hear what he was saying.

"It was always going to come to this, Angela. I can't do this anymore. I've done the best I could but it's not enough."

"If that's your way of backing out of our marriage and taking up with your floozy, Robin O'Connor, you'll have to work harder than that."

"WHAT!"

"You heard me! You and Layla cozying up to each other in that café in LA. We both saw you. How could you Rob? How bloody could you?

"Then you took her arm and waltzed off into the sunset leaving me standing in the middle of a pile of broken glass and cream, you bastard.

"How long has it been going on, anyway? Since Joe's wedding when you went back to LA?"

"Oh, hell and damnation," said a frustrated voice.

Anna had walked back up the hill and stood regarding us, feet apart and hands on her hips.

Yes, it was Anna; but at the same time, it wasn't. She'd the same bouncy curls and rosy cheeks, but when I looked into her eyes I found myself sinking, down and down, further and further, until with an effort, I pulled my gaze away. Robbie didn't have my strength. His knees buckled and he fell to the ground.

Her father hitting the floor seemed to act as some kind of trigger to Anna. I saw her shake herself and her eyes returned to the same velvet brown, gentle expression I was used to.

"Now I have your attention," she said, "You will discuss your problems like grown-ups.

"Now…" said Anna. "You first."

To Rob she said:

"You keep quiet. You'll get your turn."

I couldn't believe it – she was talking to us as if we were in Year One.

I went through the scenario of Joe's wedding and how Rob had played Darcy to Layla's Elizabeth Bennett.

"That's not fair…" began Rob.

"Shut…up!" said his daughter, "Go on, Momma."

When I explained how I'd been so upset I'd taken to my bed while his mother made fun of me, a look of empathy momentarily crossed his face.

I'd taken up painting to deal with the pain of abandonment. I'd never believed he had any true interest in me not induced by the Sisters, and thought he'd proved that by taking romantic strolls on the fells with Layla.

"Idiot…" began my husband. "I was just…"

Anna picked up a stick which conveniently lay on the ground by her foot and whacked him with it. He ducked.

I skipped over the Kilimanjaro bit except to say that was the first indication he'd given of any true commitment, and that had turned out to be a fraud.

"You're a fool," sneered Anna, "and bear in mind I'm an Empath and supposed to sympathize. Well, I don't.

"Your turn. Stop being such a sap and think out your answers carefully." she said, turning to her father.

Rob had picked himself up off the ground and was dusting off his trousers.

"My first love for Angela was a boy's crush for his playmate. She fell out of a tree and I caught her. She still broke her wrist though. Made a mess of that, too."

"Pull yourself together. Well…go on," said Anna impatiently.

"I was in constant bother with my mother for years – not without reason. In the end she kicked me out and told me not to come back until I'd made something of myself. So I went."

He told the tale of New York and how he'd been distraught at <u>Claire</u>'s death, so he'd borrowed money from Joe and gone back to Ghyll Howe for her funeral, only he was too late. It was then he'd seen me again and fallen irrevocably in love.

I sneered.

"Yes, that turned out to be typical of you Rob. You proved your mother right."

"Enough!" snapped Anna.

She was so small and yet we were standing there like naughty children, explaining ourselves.

"Now, look here, Anna…" I began in high dudgeon.

"I wouldn't if I were you," warned <u>Molly</u> who inexplicably was sitting on top of her grave stone chewing on a phantom apple. "Sorry to interrupt, Madame."

Again they chuckled together.

Our daughter fixed me with a stern eye, and I was briefly aware of that graveyard glare again.

"Continue…" she instructed Rob.

Then came the part about Joe's trip to New York and meeting his future wife Zella, and her friend Layla.

"The problem Angie seems to have with me is my relationship with Layla.

"After Joe and Zella's wedding I'd to go back early for work, and I was getting nowhere with Angela so I decided to push my luck and cozy up to Layla, to try and make her jealous. Oh, boy…did that backfire! I messed that up too – she didn't even bother seeing me off. She went to bed and pretended she was sick."

What a cow that made me sound! Worse was to come.

"In short, if the only way to win Angie was to be more like her I'd to do what my mother said. I found a way into photography in the entertainment business in

California through Zell's former boss, made a million and bought that ring."

He pointed, and I realized I'd never taken it off.

"She loved me then," he said with a sad shake of his head.

He was in tears, and I was amazed to see, so were Molly and Anna.

My God had he really believed that rubbish?

"I'm sorry I'm such a clutz," he said to me, "When it comes to you I seem not to be able to think straight. When I did the portrait I told you you switched from a child to a woman in my mind, and back again. I just never seemed to be able to think straight."

I asked permission from my daughter to speak. She agreed generously.

"What about Layla? That doesn't explain Layla and why you disappeared and ended up here."

"After Joe's wedding when we went home, she developed this thing for me and ditched her boyfriend. I swear I did nothing to encourage her."

He looked so browbeaten, but I was determined not to give in.

"Knocked off behaving like you did at Nethershaw, did you? As I recall, you walked the fells and took photographs of her – let me get this right – 'with the wind whipping her skirt about her legs and altering the color to reflect those amazing eyes?'"

Witch Ethereal

I was losing track of which of us was supposed to be jealous. It had started with him but had rapidly become me. He went on as if I hadn't spoken.

"I didn't see her for a long time and meanwhile we'd married and you were born, Anna.

"Layla had moved to Pasadena and was squatting near my studio there. We bumped, literally, into each other on the street. I hardly recognized her. She'd started drinking and then sticking needles in her arms. She was painfully thin and out of it most of the time. She said it was because I'd dumped her. As I'd never been with her, I couldn't see how that could be possible.

"Anyway, I persuaded her to go to rehab and finally she began to pull round. I found a decent little flat for her and gave her money to get back to work again. They wouldn't take her back at the studio in Hollywood, so I gave her a temporary job at the Pasadena studio. She seemed to be doing really well, but after a few months it became clear she'd come to rely on me and had no intention of moving on.

"She knew I'd married you, but I didn't tell her about Anna. She didn't care anyway. For some reason, she wanted to stay with me."

Multimillionaire with links to the music business, handsome, charming, kind and generous – why wouldn't she?

It would explain something else too - why she'd dropped out of sight when Zella tried to contact her.

Everyone was silent as he spoke. Only Anna didn't look surprised and I wondered how much of this she already knew.

"I tried – I really did – to get away. Dan found her a typing job with his agent, but both of us were embarrassed when she didn't bother turning up.

"Finally, I threatened to stop paying her rent if she didn't put some effort into getting back on track. I told her about Anna then and how I'd no intention of leaving my wife."

He looked at me with such yearning as he spoke, I forgave him on the spot.

"When I finally thought I'd extricated myself, she turned up one night at the studio when I was working late. She was high as a kite on something and threatened to kill herself if I left her. I couldn't understand it – I wasn't *with* her.

"That's when Angela and Anna saw us in the bistro and the waiter dropped the tray. I daren't leave. She'd already shown me a syringe in her purse filled with what she said was heroin and was threatening to stick it in her arm. She said there was enough there to fell an ox. I didn't know – what do I know about the drug scene?" he pleaded.

"I couldn't come back, Angie. Until I sorted out the mess I was in, I couldn't face you after what you'd seen.

"I managed to get Layla back into rehab then guessed you'd go back to Scarsdale so I dumped everything and flew here. I went to Mom's cottage at Ghyll Howe. I could feel her fury all the time I was there.

"I rode my bike back several times and stood up here with the Sisters. I'd decided if I couldn't talk you round I'd force you against one of them until you found me irresistible.

"I do, dumbass. Why else would I put up with your crap?" I screeched.

Anna was grinning, <u>Molly</u> disappeared in a golden haze and the two of us just stood gawping at each other.

"Right," said Anna, taking us both by the hand. With incredible strength she hurled us against the biggest stone.

"Get out of that!" she said clapping her hands and laughing as she walked away.

This she told us later, because neither of us heard her.

Chapter Twenty

Two Ends to the Scale

It was the following morning before we took the short walk back to Bythwaite. During our time with the Sisters we never parted once, the Ladies' pulse throbbing through our bodies, driving us mad. I think we only left because we were both so exhausted.

My face became redder the closer we got to Bythwaite – even the sheep in the pens seemed to be grinning knowingly.

And of course, the Ladies leaned forwards with smiles on all seven faces.

I grabbed Robbie's arm as we went through the farm gate.

"Do I look fit to be seen? I feel as if I've been pulled through a hedge backwards."

I fruitlessly tried to brush the bracken fronds from my hair, and wipe sheep shit off my jeans.

"I never saw you look more radiant," said my husband, bending to kiss me then enfolding me in his arms.

"Sisters or no, we can't spend the rest of our lives doing this Robin – get a grip!"

"Not you, maybe," he said, "But I think *I* could…until Gastal turns to sand. Maybe a bit longer."

I'd never seen him so full of the joy of life, even on our wedding day, when he'd made everyone there laugh uproariously with his antics.

At Bythwaite, Zella had seen us climb the hill to the Circle, so when we returned it was to eggs, mushrooms gathered from the river bank, bacon and sausage from Joe's own pigs and fried bread. She figured we'd be hungry, she said.

"Not wrong there," grinned Rob, stealing some fried bread and taking an ample bite. He nudged me and laughed at my burning face.

"Sit down or they'll think we've been up to something."

Everyone snickered at my expense, but I was so happy I didn't care a jot.

We had similar loving responses at Ghyll Howe and Scarsdale. I wouldn't say it was worth all the unhappiness and trauma – it wasn't – but it brought home to us both how much we were loved and by how many. It also served as a reminder that we didn't operate well separately.

As for my dead people. <u>Grandad Greenwood</u> had been right. The Graham Circle at Bythwaite and Scarsdale had closed. I thought I saw <u>Grandad Robert</u> once under the spreading yew in the churchyard, but the shadows were so deep I may have been wrong.

<u>Molly</u>, of course, still popped up everywhere and became Anna's 'tutor', since once or twice I saw her

whispering charms into her ear. It was impressive that a nine-year-old child could understand such sophistry from a distant whisper.

"Perhaps you should try photographing Anna and see if <u>Molly</u> turns up like <u>Claire</u> did," I suggested to Rob one day, when he'd thought Anna seemed to be having a conversation with herself. "If she could swing it for <u>Claire,</u> it should be easy for herself."

He said he wouldn't put himself out but if the occasion arose, he might just do that.

It was past time we returned home to Reina del Sur. For the first time that is what I truly felt it was.

We were in our souls husband and wife again and could tackle the problem of our daughter together. I thought Anna would be gentle with us until we understood, but after the drubbing she gave us at the Sisters I wasn't entirely confident of that.

It was even harder knowing, according to my great grandmother, we were bringing up Wicca royalty. I was relying on <u>Molly</u> to explain that to us, and hoped and prayed she wouldn't disappear too.

Rob had two major tasks when we got back, both of which I thought I could help him with.

A businessman can't just up and leave without consequences and that's just what he'd done. Fortunately his staff were exemplary and pretty much used to coping alone.

I brought the paperwork from all three studios to go through at home, while Rob caught up on outstanding orders and saw to any prima donnas with disjointed noses.

The second was more difficult and he definitely wanted me there. Layla.

He made his last call of the day at the Pasadena studio. He wanted her to know he and I were a unit, and he had no interest in any kind of romantic link – never had.

She was in the accounts office when we arrived. Rob thought it might be better for me to talk to her alone. He thought both he and I together might be a bit overwhelming in view of what had to be said, and she might be a bit less hysterical if I spoke to her without him being there.

In any case, he said, he needed to talk to his manager Alan Dean, about any problems arising during his absence.

Al organized us both a coffee, and the look on his face as he handed the cup to me spoke volumes.

In her office, Layla was kneeling on the floor sorting through the bottom drawer of a filing cabinet when I entered and didn't immediately look up. When I remembered the cool chick who fixed Zella's dress and walked the fells with Rob, I was flabbergasted by her appearance.

She was so thin.

She was wearing a low-necked t-shirt and her breastbones stuck out with shadowed hollows above, her cheeks were sunken and her beautiful hair lank, and badly cared for. But worst were the blemishes under her skin which spoke of addiction. Was she using again?

When she saw me Layla got up, put the papers she'd taken on the cabinet top and waited. She stood her ground but her eyes were wary. She was figuring out how to play this, so I took the initiative. I hoped she would find my tone conciliatory.

"I do know what's been happening, Layla. Rob's told me everything."

"Did he send you rather than come himself?" she asked.

"He's talking to Al. Would you like me to fetch him?"

I knew full well that would go down like a lead brick with Rob, but fortunately she didn't call my bluff, just stared at me blankly.

"Did he tell you everything?" she asked.

Her demeanor altered and she became aggressive.

"Did he tell you he had me over that filing cabinet and… and Al's desk and…he gave me this."

She picked up her purse from an adjoining desk and scrabbled about in the bottom of if for a moment or two, then held out her hand. In her palm was an engagement ring."

"There'd have to be a divorce and everything, so he told me I couldn't wear it just yet."

It was at this point I knew Robbie was on the level. His style was Kilimanjaro not Gastal Cragg. It was sadly pathetic.

Slow tears began to seep down her cheeks.

"I'm sorry to hurt anyone," she whispered.

"I think the only person you've hurt is yourself, Layla. Rob and I were at loggerheads for a short while, but it resolved itself with Anna's help. Anna's Anastasia, our daughter. She's nine and has to be our primary concern."

It could have been more tactfully put but there was a limit to my philanthropy.

There was loud male laughter from the next room so I assumed Rob and Alan were winding up their business meeting.

"Please," Layla implored, "Please, tell him I don't want to see him. I need to be somewhere quiet. Somewhere alone. Please.

"I need to think…to do some serious thinking. I'd like to take a long walk. I need to smell the trees, hear the rushing water and be with the mountains."

Perhaps that *would* be for the best. She might come to some conclusions which would allow her to move on. I gave her the rest of the afternoon off and smuggled her out of the back door into the narrow concrete alley, which skirted the length of the building and opened directly onto the parking lot.

Chapter Twenty-one
Moriarty to Rob's Sherlock

Rob walked through the door with Al, still laughing.

He'd his shirt-sleeves rolled to the elbow and his jacket slung over one shoulder. He parked himself on the edge of Layla's desk and grinned at me.

"Where's Layla?" he asked, looking round, "I wanted to ask her if she could work a couple of late evenings to catch up with some routine typing. Where is she?"

"She was a bit upset after our chat so I gave her the afternoon off. She said she needed a bit of fresh air to think. She mentioned mountains and trees and…rushing water. Must have been feeling overwrought."

It seemed to be important to Layla so I stopped to think.

"Is there a park nearby? Perhaps that's what she meant."

"The closest is quite a distance away. There's the Angeles Forest. That's less than a half hour's drive."

"There's Millard Falls" suggested Al uneasily, "That's got rushing water. You can drive into the mountains from Altadena then it's only about a mile or so to hike."

Rob grabbed my hand and bolted for the parking lot. He opened the passenger door and all but threw me inside.

"I can't take the chance she's not going to top herself," he said, as he swerved the car into reverse, and took the road toward the mountains.

Rob had a small pile of speeding tickets stacked on the hall table at Reina del Sur - speeding was natural to him. This time he was in a panic. I was afraid to distract him, so didn't speak.

That was fine until we hit the mountain track then I'd to shut my eyes round the hairpin bends. Rob pulled into a viewing point after which the road became a trail blocked off by a barrier.

He helped me out, dropped my hand and fled up the track. I did my best to follow but he was out of sight before I could catch him.

The start of the trail was rocky, and in places tipped with the mountain's slope. It was hard going but soon evened out to a sandy path crossed by streams narrow enough to jump.

I saw Rob haring up the path half way up a slope in front of me. Then I lost him. By this time I was thoroughly winded so leaned against a tree to catch my breath. I could only follow at a walk.

By the time I neared the top of the slope, the sound of rushing water became deafening.

I found Robin sitting on the bank to one side of a gigantic waterfall – not broad, but forced between two cliff-sides, narrow and precipitous. It dropped, I estimated - fifty feet, maybe more – into a broad rocky pool, which incongruously reminded me of the river at Scarsdale.

He was rocking backwards and forwards with his hands over his face. When I sat beside him and pulled them away to speak to him, I was crushed by the grief in his eyes. He was inconsolable and at first I'd no idea why. Then the truth dawned and I looked at him in horror. She'd carried out the threat she'd made should he leave.

I yelled at the top of my voice over the deafening roar of the torrent:

"PLEASE TELL ME SHE DIDN'T!"

My throat closed with the effort and emotion, and I took a step forward to see what he had seen, but her body had lodged in a cleft in the rock out of sight, beneath where we stood. Poor Rob had seen her jump, too late to reach her.

He leapt to his feet and pulled me backwards, afraid I might fall, and I tumbled hard on the rocky ground, rolling over in pain.

He rocked me in his arms and I twisted my fingers in his shirt and wept with him.

I can't recall how long we sat there, grieving for the wasted life which had been Layla Wilson's, but eventually Rob said:

"There's a camp site and Visitors' Center near where I parked the car. They'll have a phone to contact the police."

"Shouldn't we go and pull her out of the water?"

"She's just fallen forty feet down a rocky slope. I don't want to subject you to what you might see. The authorities will probably want to check things out anyway."

Who could have foreseen this? Of all people on earth who didn't deserve this disaster it was Robin O'Connor.

I was suddenly angry with Layla, and concluded that suicide must be the most selfish of actions, one which had no thought for anyone else but the perpetrator; no thought for the grief and guilt left behind – even Sherlock Holmes wept for the watery death of the wicked Moriarty.

"Could I have done anything, Angie? Was I too cruel? You and Anna are my life. I'd already stretched things to the limit with you. I couldn't take any more chances."

"No, it absolutely wasn't your fault she took to drink and drugs and chose to live in dumpsters. It wasn't your fault she took your generosity and used it against you. In no way was any of this your fault!"

I was getting more furious by the second.

He pulled me into a hug.

"You're good at death. This is the third and you've aced it every time."

I supposed that was a compliment of sorts.

Once we were back home, he ate nothing, and lay on the couch with his head in my lap trembling for three days.

After that, I persuaded him to walk with me along the beach in the early hours when there was no-one about, and no sound but the peaceful lull of waves, their crests the only visible thing but for the glorious wheel of the milky way.

Rob laid back to watch it, until the horizon gave way to a stupefying sunrise, which turned our skins to gold and made inky silhouettes of the pilings of the pier.

At weekends, or when Rob wasn't working, this became a habit of ours. We figured if Anna had Molly's protection, she'd have no problem with a burglar.

I didn't push Rob back to work.

To say his life had been a train-wreck over the past few years would have been to understate things. It said something for him that he had begun to smile again – even to laugh. Al Dean and Steve Speirs at Pasadena and Huntington were more than competent and Don Fargo, who'd taken over the Santa Monica studio had been given a whopping pay-rise so was doing his best to please.

But eventually Rob thought going back was the right thing to do, especially when Danny Charlton rang with more work. Rob considered Dan a good friend and always did his work personally. As he was the best there was in LA, personal attention from Rob O'Connor was a compliment.

It always made me smile when I remembered the day Danny had first met Rob, before he had made his mark, and Deidra, Rob's mother, had adopted Dan as an extra son, clipping Robbie round the ear for being cheeky – he was thirty years old at the time.

Danny had been a guest at our wedding along with the guys from the band Lakota. Rob had made many friends amongst his clients.

A few months later, when I was rinsing out a coffee cup and gazing lackadaisically out of the kitchen window, I was struck by a sudden thought.

"Anna, did you know anything about Layla before she died?"

"Possibly," she said. "Depends what you mean by 'anything'."

"Don't sass me Anna. Answer my question, please. Did you know what was happening to her?"

"Of course," she said, as if it had been a ridiculous question, "The Manteis tell me what's going on."

"What?"

"The Manteis – the seers. They're a family, called seers because they see everything. Well, most things anyway," she said with a crafty grin. "There are three of them – one guy who sounds quite old and two girls. Theia's about my age – she has visions. They talk in my head like Molly."

"So what did they see with Layla?"

I was beginning to lose patience.

"They saw she was a pain in the arse for Daddy, but it was Molly who encouraged her to jump in the water. She felt how heartbroken you both were and it bothered her."

"She did WHAT!"

"She told her to jump in the water."

She became aware of my horror and looked uncertain.

"It seemed a good idea at the time," she said, regaining her confidence. "I won't let anyone hurt my Dad. He'd have no idea what was going on."

I clenched my teeth in fury.

"You mean you had a hand in this too? You tell Molly I want to see her," I ordered. "Today."

Chapter Twenty-three

Molly and the Lady

"You'll stop worrying sooner or later," said my daughter who apparently could mind-read amongst her other accomplishments.

"I wouldn't bank on that," I snapped. "Teaching people a lesson is one thing but making them jump off waterfalls is quite different. You can't kill people Anna, no matter how they annoy you. It's not allowed."

Puddy strolled into the room, twined himself round Anna's legs and regarded me balefully. I was yelling at his mistress – that wasn't allowed either.

I'd no time to consider that at the moment – I needed to tackle Molly. I hadn't thought being beyond the Veil gave her permission to hurt people over here. As far as I understood it, her job was to care for us. Perhaps it was more complicated than I thought. Perhaps she had to protect us at any cost. Because of Anna?

Molly woke me in the middle of the night and scared the crap out of me. Rob slept on, snoring softly.

She put her finger to her lips then beckoned me to the garden. I was seething.

"Anna says you want to see me – about that Layla, Lynda, Lulu…oh, whatever her name was. It's not important."

"It bloody-well is! She's…"

"…was…" corrected Molly.

"She was a person – a human being with feelings. You can't just kill her off because she's in the way. Have you forgotten the way of things this side of the curtain?"

"It's a Veil, and no, I'd have given her a shove whichever side. She was destroying things between you and Robin. The Lady wouldn't have that. "

"What Lady?"

"Your Lady – Anna. When did you become so dim, Angela? You're very slow on the uptake today."

"Don't start, Molly. You cause trouble everywhere you go. You're not starting on Anna…I won't allow it. So far, you've messed with Grandad Robert, Claire, Mum, Dad, me and Rob. You're not getting Anna as well."

Her face creased in annoyance.

"Not me alone, fool! The Sisters, too."

"The Sisters are lumps of rock with some nice stories attached. What the hell can *they* do?"

"I think you already know the answer to *that*," she said with a giggle, and made a bzzz sound. "In any case, they weren't always lumps of rock, and unless I'm vastly mistaken, one day they won't be again."

I changed tack:

"What about Rob? He believes in <u>Claire</u>. It's a combination of a photo he took, and the fact he so vividly feels her presence. On the other hand he thinks the rest of you are figments of the Greenwood imagination, and the thought of Anna being of the blood terrifies him."

"You'd think if he understood about <u>Claire</u> he'd have figured the rest of us out."

"Why? He doesn't know what a first class troublemaker you are, and his Dad taught him exactly why a corpse is called 'a stiff', given that he was somewhat cold at the time."

I thought of my lovely <u>Grandad Greenwood</u> grinning at me over the wheatfield wall.

"Never mind Robin. He's easily dealt with. Leave him to me. Shh, he's awake," she warned.

My <u>great grandmother, Molly Carrick Graham</u>, disappeared in a rapidly fading haze.

"Don't you dare harm him!" I whispered after her, in alarm.

Rob had come into the garden, concerned I was standing in the middle of the lawn talking to myself. I told him I was singing – in the middle of the garden at three in the morning. He must still have been half-asleep because he didn't argue, he just hugged me and made some romantic reference to the moon, which was especially bright, a witches' moon.

As he bent his head to kiss me, over his shoulder I caught a glimpse of Anna standing at the window, smiling lovingly at us both.

I waited for some kind of response, but Molly didn't come back and Anna refused point blank to discuss either her or Layla.

I called Bythwaite to let Zella know about the tragedy. She shed a few tears, but her time with Layla was long ago and far away. She now had an adored family in a land of fairytale cottages and family ghosts and had no wish to remember her past.

It was such a heartbreaking situation. We could find no family for Layla, and her addiction had got rid of any friends. Zella was long gone, and she seemed to have been entirely alone.

As a comfort for Rob, I paid for her cremation and we scattered her ashes at the one place we knew she'd found some peace, into the waves at Huntington Beach, where she'd once walked with Kris.

Such adversities – as this with Layla - always seemed to concentrate Anna's mind, and she focused on controlling her abilities even further. Puddy helped with this. From time to time I found them in the livingroom or garden. Anna had the cat on her knee, holding her quite tightly, sitting with her eyes closed. Her lips moved rhythmically as if she was chanting or singing to herself.

After our daughter seemed to have taken control of her life for a few months, I decided to enroll her in High School. Rob was enthusiastic and she was happy about it, but only made one friend, Cam's daughter Catherine. If she gave the other students and teachers the 'royalty' act, I couldn't say I was surprised, but she seemed happy enough, and I didn't doubt Rob when he said it was better for her to have company of her own age.

"If not of her intelligence," he couldn't resist saying with pride.

One day a few years later, during which time nothing of great significance had occurred, and when Anna must have been about fifteen, Rob had dashed off to work, roaring down the drive in his Corvett. I decided Anna was old enough and had proved her self-control so it was time to broach the question of my meeting with Molly all that time ago.

"I was wondering if you still heard from Molly."

"Most days - because you worry about him, about Dad."

"Did you know, after Layla died, Molly came to see me?"

"Yes, I told her to. You seemed to think it was important."

All those parents who complained about awkward teenagers should try having an awkward teen who was a powerful witch – more than that, Wicca royalty.

Later that same day, I saw Anna, Puddy in her arms, staring thoughtfully at the portrait photograph Rob had taken of me, and hung on the dining room wall the night she warned him to tell me about Layla.

He'd somehow fixed it so I looked like Rita Hayworth - he was a very talented man.

"Do you think Dad would take some pictures of me and Katy? I'd like to have one for Cam – and you, too."

"He'd enjoy that," I said. "He's mentioned it a time or two."

"We can do it Sunday. Dan'll be there too. Perhaps he and Nik would like to be in them."

"I haven't seen Cam in an age. It'll be good to see her again," I said.

"No," she said shortly, and went to her room.

Chapter Twenty-four

Anna and Molly as One

So that Sunday afternoon, with my husband and daughter at Linden Reach with my friend Cam, I found myself at a loose end. It was a lovely day – not too hot - so I went to watch the surfers.

There was quite a swell. Boys were there in droves, carrying their boards to the beach or zooming about the promenade on bicycles. Girls, in the shortest of short shorts, roller-skated along concrete walkways next to a beach heaving with sunbathers and swimmers.

I bought an ice cream from a nearby van and had just sat down on a bench to watch, when there was the soft 'pop' I was so familiar with.

"Sod off, Molly," I said from the corner of my mouth, "If anybody sees me talking to myself, they'll have me committed."

"Not stopping. Just to let you know I fixed it, as I said."

Although Anna said she heard Molly most days, it was years since she'd been to see me – shortly after Layla died, and Anna had told me she'd been responsible for the plunge to her death over a waterfall.

I knew I should remember what she was talking about but my mind was a blank. What had Molly done wrong she needed to fix? Time has no meaning for those beyond the Veil so whatever it was might have happened long ago. I supposed it was even possible it had happened to Mum.

I threw my ice cream paper in a trash can and went home.

Rob was in his dark-room humming to himself and working on the pictures he'd taken that morning at Linden Reach. Dan had been there too, and Rob had managed to get good shots of all of them.

Anna had stayed behind with Katy, so for once Rob and I had the house to ourselves.

"Be there in half an hour," Rob said, as I purred sexily. "Shut the door – you're letting the light in."

If ever there was a passion killer it was being told someone had time for you in half an hour. I said so. Loudly. Through the shut door.

When I peeked in a little later he was still distracted and pegging prints to a line strung across one corner of the room.

I gently separated the pictures. They were pretty good.

"I like this one of Anna and Katy," I said, peering at it through the ultra-violet light dimmed by daylight from the open door."

I unpegged the still-damp photo and took it to the light to examine it. I had wondered if <u>Molly</u> would repeat her trick of allowing Rob to see <u>Claire,</u> but the photograph was just that, a very good print of friends. The other shots were better still, taken covertly as they chatted and laughed.

As I sorted through the pictures, it came to me how like Molly Anna looked. Mum used to say I was her double as a small child, and Anna appeared to be the same, except she had Rob's curls which tumbled in profusion down her back and framed her face.

One picture was of Anna on her own, hair carefully arranged over one shoulder and head turned three-quarters of the way towards the viewer. As I gazed at it, the head turned gradually, the face looked me straight in the eye, then very slowly one eye closed in a wink. Molly! I blinked and when I looked back the photo was normal again. Just a very charming picture of a lovely girl.

For the other framed photo, Rob chose a picture of himself. It was the one photo Anna had taken, or it would have been a very unusual thing for him to do.

The head faced the opposite direction from the first, so the two photos complimented each other.

He'd developed both with a sepia tint and faded the outline so they looked dreamy and idealistic.

I'd have thought I'd imagined the wink had it been anyone but Molly but I knew I hadn't. I just hoped to hell Rob hadn't noticed; but then he wouldn't, he'd never seen Molly, and as far as he was concerned the picture was of Anna.

"I never noticed before, how like you Anna is," said Rob, looking over my shoulder, "She's a real Greenwood."

"No, she looks like the Grahams, my mother's family. She's got your gorgeous curls though."

I turned and ruffled his hair affectionately. How was it we'd lost touch? We were made for each other. All the other people in our lives – dead or alive - were just interruptions in a perfect vista of togetherness.

The frames for the pictures he'd made himself – narrow and of natural wood– were tucked away in a cabinet in the darkroom.

"Go away," he smiled. "I don't want you to see them until they're hung."

It was a couple of hours later, when Anna had arrived home from the Chiltons, the grand unveiling happened. During that time Rob had dried, cropped and framed the pictures and hung them on the dining room wall.

"It's missing one of you, Momma," said Anna, studying them critically.

"That's a work in progress," said her Dad laughing, "Can't decide which of the hundred thousand to choose."

He walked over to the photos to correct the hang, When his back was turned Anna looked at me sharply.

"That's not me," she mouthed.

"Talk later."

I loved the picture of Robbie. Anna had caught his romanticism perfectly. The shot had been taken from the side with his head turned away, gazing off into the distance. It made me think of the day I'd seen him silhouetted against the sky at Scarsdale when the Stones had conquered my resistance, and he reminded me of Heathcliffe.

Once Rob was out of earshot Anna cornered me about the photograph.

"What's wrong with the picture? He pointed the camera at me – I saw him. How has it changed to someone else? Who is it?"

"<u>Molly</u>. She's an expert at this. The only reason Dad believes anything about us at all is that <u>Molly</u> fixed it for him to see our aunt <u>Claire</u> when he didn't seem able to get over her death. She could only do it through a photographic image."

"So why's she infected this photo?"

I liked her choice of words.

"Why don't you ask her next time you tune in? Perhaps this picture was meant for you."

"I'll do that."

Chapter Twenty-five

Rob Comes Face to Face With His Worst Nightmare

Cam Chilton was a very special lady, beautiful, accomplished. That I wasn't keen on some of her friends wasn't her fault.

One of them, Lena Michaels, Anna had told me, was a hostile. That is to say she was a wisher of bad luck simply by touch. She had two children, who although unpleasant, didn't seem to have inherited her curse.

These two scared the hell out of Anna's friend, Cam's gentle daughter Catherine – they were inveterate bullies.

This had the makings of a slowly evolving disaster. Anna didn't love many people, but Katy was her special friend and she would always defend her.

Anna, who had done her level best to co-operate with the control of her ever-strengthening powers, came to me one day and said:

"You know you said I shouldn't kill people because they're a pain in the ass? Is it okay to give them a good slap?"

"Depends. What's happened?"

"Sandy Michaels pushed Katy down the stairs at school and her ankle's in plaster."

"Okay but don't go overboard. Make sure the punishment fits the crime – no more."

A couple of days later, I had an irate phone call from the school Principal asking me why Anna had suspended Sandy from the school roof.

Apparently, she'd been tied there by her ankle and wrist and two or three very nervous pupils had blamed it on Anna.

I tried not to laugh – truly I did – especially when confronted by a very self-satisfied daughter.

"It was only a sprain," Anna said. "She broke bones in Katy's foot," then with defiance. "I'm not sorry in the least."

This little episode was the beginning of a disastrous domino effect.

Marcus Michaels, Sandy's brother, had seen Anna march Sandy up the spiral stairs to the top of the tower, twine a leather strap round her ankle and wrist, then lift her – he couldn't say how because she seemed to float through the air…"

It was at this point his story became less convincing…

"Sandy began to swing from the castle bits of the tower."

I couldn't fault Anna. She hadn't thrown her off the roof as she could very easily have done. She'd made the punishment fit the crime by only spraining her ankle. That she'd sprained her wrist too was incidental.

Rob's reaction was to be expected:

"Tosh! How could a fifteen-year-old girl with no muscles hoist that little fatty over the wall. It's not possible."

When he'd marched out of the room in a rage, I asked Anna:

"So, back to square one. What am I going to say to your teacher? Marcus saw you."

"Just tell her it was impossible like Dad said, and he must have imagined it."

Blaming the whole thing on a seemingly innocent Anna, who walked round for a month looking aggrieved, didn't do much for the popularity of the Michaels children. Anna was too strong a character to care, and as is the nature of things, she seemed to pick up followers.

It meant that the whole school understood Katy was under Anna's protection, so she was left alone.

It also meant the Michael's children were obliged to swallow their bile. Repeatedly. Until the only person on earth to believe them was their mother, Lena.

Anna and I knew Lena was Wicca but weakly so – she needed to touch to hex.

After the incident between Katy and the Michaels children, I became aware of Lena on several other occasions. Each time seemed to be followed by a variety of disasters of more or less severity.

At a Long Beach barbeque, she helped a guy with a surf-board to a burger. As he took it from her hand, he burned himself, and shouted out with pain, dropping his board into the embers, where it sizzled then burst into flames.

On another occasion, she was helping a mother with a baby down steps in the park, when the woman's hand slipped on the stroller and it tipped sideways, bumping and jolting, flipping over and over, down two full flights.

It was fortunate the mother was spry and the baby not strapped in or there would have been serious injury to both. As it was, the screaming baby took a crack to its forehead which quickly swelled and turned purple. The woman skinned her arm from elbow to wrist.

Lena saw me sitting at a picnic table watching, and she glared. Anna was with me and I knew for certain, had she not been, the child would have died. At the bottom of the steps, for no apparent reason, the mother fell again and twisted her ankle.

The Michael's children, who both seemed glued to their mother's skirt, stood at the top of the steps and grinned with satisfaction at the upset their mother had caused. Their smirks rapidly faded, however. They'd been on the receiving end of Anna's anger already.

Their mother followed their line of sight and scowled at Anna, who stared back, her eyes' dark with menace.

"I'll go see the lady home," said Anna, as Lena collected her brats and left.

Cam and Nik had invited us and some other friends to dinner at their home. Lena was also a guest as was Dan Charlton's fiancé Jill. Dan was away so we'd collected her en route to introduce her.

Lena was in the hallway as Jill, Rob and I took off our coats. She glared at me but smiled ingratiatingly at Rob and Jill, who returned the greeting, unaware of what she was, and before I could stop them, both had shaken her hand. I saw Rob give an involuntary shudder, then turn and crash into a tall table holding a house plant. The whole lot came crashing down. The pot smashed and compost and plant scattered in all directions.

Rob, Jill and the rest of the company were too concerned with picking up the pieces to notice the smirk on Lena's face. But I saw it and could only think of one course of action which would mitigate the problem without causing too much distress.

"Cam, would you mind if I brought Anna over? I know I didn't give you warning but she's alone in the house and it's making me nervous."

"Sure. She can have a sleep-over with Katy. She'd love that."

I telephoned Anna to come over. I was puzzled by the speed with which she arrived. She must have already been on her way, because whereas the journey should have taken almost an hour by taxi, she was there in half that.

Cam looked surprised, Lena apprehensive.

"<u>Molly</u>?" I whispered in Anna's ear as I bent to kiss her.

"No. Theia Manteis. You remember, the seer."

These beings were new to me, but at that moment I was glad of their intervention.

"Since you were in the house alone, I asked Cam if you could come over and keep Katy company. I thought you might both enjoy that," I said brightly for the whole room to hear.

"I wasn't alone. Puddy was…"

She stopped when I surreptitiously stepped on her toe.

"Thanks, Cam. It'll be great. I'll go find her," she said instead.

"Don't go far – you'll know why," I whispered again.

She nodded but gave Lena a hard stare as she turned away. Anna wanted her to understand there would be reprisals.

But the hex had already been made and Lena didn't have the strength to take it back. Anna would be needed.

Cam had made a wonderful meal. She was a keen cook so it was all her own work. Nik was a solicitous host and made sure our wine glasses were kept topped up.

Jill had been introduced to everyone, and being a confident person, Cam and her friends took to her right away. Lena, I noticed, held back and took little part in the conversation.

The anticipated disaster happened just as the tarte tatin was being placed on the table.

Jill had reached out to take a bowl of whipped cream from one of the other guests, when the tassels on the long lace shawl she was wearing, wrapped tightly round the intricate back of her Hepplewhite chair. Rob saw what had happened and jumped up to help her, accidentally knocking the chair sideways. Jill was thrown to the floor, with the shawl tied to the chair back still wound around her neck. Her face turned red then blue as the air was cut off from her lungs.

Everyone tried to untie her, which only made matters worse. Before Cam could return from the kitchen with scissors it was all over. I heard the crack as her neck snapped.

There was a deathly hush as we all stood from the table. Cam and Nik froze in horror.

"I'll call an ambulance," said Nik, then as she was clearly dead, "and the cops."

A shout came from the top of the stairs and we turned to see Anna and Katy standing there.

"Cut her free Dad, then put her in Momma's room. Both of you stop in there with her. I'm coming.

I grabbed the scissors from Cam's rigid hand and began to saw at the fringes of the shawl.

"Nothing can be done Anna. She's already gone," said Nik.

"DO AS YOU'RE TOLD! NOW…before it's too late… NOW!"

Everyone had frozen in mid-action, shocked at orders from a furious sixteen year old.

All that is except me, Rob and, not surprisingly, Lena.

Rob was galvanized into action.

He picked Jill up from the floor, balancing her head against his chest and bolted for the door, with me hot on his heels. Anna tumbled into the room after us, shut the door and locked it.

"Put her face-down on the bed, Dad. Cut the rest of the shawl loose, Momma. Oh hell, I hope this will work. The best I've done until now has been a raccoon at the zoo. Bastard thing bit me when it came to."

"What are you going to do, Anna?" asked her father, who was hoping against hope the answer in his head wasn't the truth.

"Straighten her neck Momma."

"What the hell are you doing Anna?" yelled my husband. "You're going to get us all locked up."

There was a pounding on the door.

"Do as I say – NOW – while there's still time. Save the questions for later."

"Do whatever she says, Rob. Trust me, she knows what she's doing."

I hoped to hell she did – a raccoon and a human being are hardly comparable.

"No, they're not," she said, reading my mind. "Just pray. Hold her head Dad."

Rob was ashen and for a moment I thought he would pass out. He wasn't going to be able to winkle his way out of believing this easily.

"For heaven's sake, Robin – get hold of yourself! You've seen her repair a bird. This can't be that much different."

Along with the other two I instantly realized what a stupid remark that was.

Anna rubbed her hands over her forehead then began gently to feel for the break in Jill's spine. I saw her nod to herself once she'd located it. Anna pressed down and curled her fingers round Jill's neck until she left nail marks in the soft skin.

It was at that point I relaxed. Molly was there with her eyes closed and her hand on Anna's shoulder.

Not only Molly, but a group of other women of various ages and different modes of dress. Each, like Molly, had closed eyes and the oldest amongst them also bowed their heads. I could see their lips moving.

More pounding on the door, but this time with the sound of splintering wood.

"Pray hard now – all of you!"

"All?" said Rob. "All three?"

"Shut up and pray," I said.

The door gave way just as Jill rolled over on the bed and sat up.

"Thank God for that," said Anna. "For a minute there I thought, despite the cavalry," she thumbed over her shoulder where the crones had been, "I thought it wasn't going to happen."

Chapter Twenty-six
Coming to Terms With a Nightmare

Two cops fell through the door in time to see my husband collapse and Jill raised from the dead, although they weren't aware of that.

Anna, looking thoroughly exhausted, made some excuse and ran off to find Katy and go to bed.

All the other guests bar one, most of whom had also heard the crack of Jill's neck, stood in the doorway, stunned.

Lena was in the hall when I dashed to the kitchen for a glass of water to revive Robin. She was putting on her coat and flung an elaborate velvet wrap over her shoulders.

As I ran past I noticed Anna standing at the top of the stairs, her face a mask. I paused for a moment to watch, as Lena turned blue in the face, the scarf pulling tighter and tighter. When she began to sink to her knees, I reminded Anna of the presence of the LAPD in the bedroom, and suggested they might not appreciate her help with their job. She released Lena laughing, and taking Katy's hand, skipped back up the stairs to bed. Empathy worked two ways it would seem, one way for the sufferer and the polar opposite for the perpetrator.

Jill had helped a shaky Robbie to his feet and they were sitting side by side on the bed.

I wondered if she'd been dead long enough to catch a quick peek beyond the Veil but she looked so cheerful I decided she hadn't.

Rob took the glass of water from my hand and looked at me shame-faced. Jill had been dead, he'd merely fainted, but he got the water. He hesitantly offered her a drink but she said no.

We were the last to leave, and as she helped me on with my coat, Cam asked:

"What the hell happened there? Unless Anna can raise the dead what did she do in that room with the door locked. We all heard Jill's neck crack."

This was no rhetorical question. It was as if there was something particular she needed to know. I could think of no response but:

"Dislocated shoulder. You know what teenagers are like. She's been doing first-aid at school so thought she'd give it a go."

That didn't even sound convincing to me, so heaven only knows what Cam thought.

We left Anna with Katy and ran Jill home. She smiled sweetly as she climbed out of the car – she was a lovely girl, just Danny's type.

"Thank you for a wonderful evening. It was great to meet your friends. Perhaps we can all do lunch sometime?"

"Great idea – I'll mention it to Cam. Meantime, I'd better get my husband home before he passes out again."

Rob looked too frail to care.

At home, I got Rob some Tums for his stomach and Paracetamol for his head.

"I'll be fine. Just give me a minute," he said, sounding like the invalid in a Victorian novel. I made a nice cup of comforting English tea.

"There's no way of avoiding this any longer, Rob. You've done your level best to follow the example set by my Dad and Uncle Joe. You're not as adept as they are at ignoring the obvious, so let's get it over with.

"We got over the thing with Layla which was horrendous – and partly Anna's fault. We can do this too."

He sat quietly.

I told him about me and Mum with <u>Molly</u>, the Seven Sisters – a little of which he'd experienced – Auntie <u>Claire</u> and my <u>Grandad Robert</u>. In fact, I told him everything up to and including Anna's birth. He was going to hate what came next.

"If you remember I also told you I'd taken Anna to see <u>Molly</u> after you'd gone back to work and left us at Scarsdale. You were furious. <u>Molly</u> was the most powerful witch I'd ever met but Anna is in a different league.

"<u>Molly</u> says she's Wicca royalty and calls her the Lady – always has. There's something about their relationship I haven't figured out yet…" I said, brow furrowed.

"…Never mind. You managed to ignore it when she brought that little bird back to life, but you can't shrug your daughter off quite so easily this time. You can question her when she comes back if you like, but she knows every word we're saying. She has a family of friends called Manteis. They're people from the other side of the Veil. She's especially close to their daughter Theia, who has visions apparently. Anyway, they're seers, which according to Anna, means they see everything as it's happening."

"What's the Veil?" he asked weakly. "And are you saying Anna can raise the dead? You are, aren't you?"

"As <u>Molly</u> explained it to me, the Veil is the barrier between this world and the world of the dead. It seems Anna is the first person in two thousand years who can flit through the Veil at will and manipulate both sides."

"Oh God," he said, rubbing both hands over his face and looking strained.

"I suggest you speak to her. She can explain it in more detail than I can. Go to bed, Rob. You look beat."

I cuddled up beside him on the bed quilt, and watched the shadows cross his face as he tried to assimilate what he'd been told.

"If it helps, you should know Anna's already told me, of all the people on earth, you are the one she would protect with her life. Partly because she thinks all this is beyond you."

"Make love to me," he said miserably. "I need to know that's normal, at least."

"That's not normal," I said, "It's beyond wonderful."

In the hypnotic beauty of the early morning hours, we sat on the soft sands of the beach and watched the sun rise.

Without taking his eyes from the dazzling splendor, Rob said:

"Please tell me there's nothing weird in this."

The sweep of his arm encompassed the glory of the natural vista before him.

"When I was overawed by the strangeness of my life, I always used to walk the Fells," I said slowly, "They have been the same since the world came into being, eternal and immutable. Here, the same can be said of the sun and sea and the mountains above Pasadena."

We walked home hand in hand. At the bottom of our drive he said:

"Please don't think I'm not worth your while because I don't understand."

"Robin O'Connor, you've been there for me my entire life. Sometimes I've thought you were my only link with reality. I love you with all my magical soul…"

Then I scooted up the drive before he could catch me.

Over breakfast Robbie said, serious:

"How shall I approach this with Anna? She already thinks I'm ridiculous – dim even. I don't want to make it any more obvious," Rob said, stirring his breakfast tea.

"She doesn't think that at all. Perhaps it's best explained by saying you're like a clever but uneducated child. All you need is to have the facts explained – you'll soon get used to it."

"Is that supposed to make me feel better? An uneducated child?"

At that moment, Anna rolled in from Cam's.

"Who's an uneducated child?" she asked kicking off her shoes and climbing onto the stool next to her Dad.

"I am, apparently," said her father, looking morose, "Seems the world has been spinning without me. Momma thinks you'll be better able to explain things to me."

"You'll soon get the hang of it. I'll give you a few starters. Right?

"First – Molly is Momma's great grandmother – she died sometime in the nineteen-thirties, I think. She's a fairly powerful witch.

"Most witches are restricted to location and people they've known in life, but Molly was head of her Coven…"

That was news to me.

Witch Ethereal

"...so has the power to flit about all over – she even comes to California. We speak almost daily, but only Momma can see her."

"Will *I* see her?"

"No, of course not," said Anna impatiently. "Are you a woman?...or a witch?"

"Well obviously the answer's no!"

"Stop it, Anna," I said when Rob began to look rattled by her attitude. "Explain properly or go to your room."

Her expression said, 'I'd like to see you make me', but I faced her down and eventually she dropped the teen-age-itis and said:

"Oh, alright,"

"Who has these abilities?" asked Robbie.

"All Molly's female line – Grandma and me. Momma sees dead people."

"She does, doesn't she?" he said weakly, being forced to face facts I'd been trying to ram down his throat for decades.

"She sees Molly, Momma's auntie Claire…"

"Yes, I know about her. She sent me a photograph."

"She did?" It was Anna's turn to look surprised. "Damn, isn't that the coolest?

"Claire's not related but she's a special case, she'll just confuse you, so I'll explain her later when you've got a handle on the rest of it. Then there's Momma's grandad, Robert Graham – Grannie Meg's Dad - and her other grandad, Josh Greenwood - Grandpa Guy's

Dad. They can't do the hocus-pocus because they're guys so they're second-rate."

"Anna…!" I warned.

"Sorry," she said quickly.

"Is there more?" asked Rob, dismayed. "You'd better tell me – there can't be anything worse than realizing your daughter can raise the dead."

"Oh, that's just the beginning," Anna said cheerfully, settling herself on her stool.

It was now she really did overstep the mark with her Dad. For a moment I thought she'd killed him. He went as white as a ghost if you'll pardon the analogy.

"<u>Molly</u> sees your mother and father quite often too. <u>Grandma O'Connor</u> won't come and see me. She says if you find out it'll scare the crap out of you, so for now at least, she'll keep to herself."

Rob looked shellshocked, whether from the thought of his mother's reappearance, or his daughter's colorful language, I couldn't say.

"Can we stop there?" he said and went to lay down on our bed completely blitzed. The rest of us had grown up with everything he'd been told over the past hour or so.

He'd had to take it in one.

Chapter Twenty-seven
Learning to Live with a Princess

I warned Anna not to pursue this until her Dad had had time to work things through in his own mind.

"Jeez," she said, "He's going to have apoplexy when he hears details about me."

"Absolutely right… 'apoplexy'? How did you come by that word?"

"<u>Molly</u> says it often."

"Yes," I said, rolling my eyes, "she would."

It was perhaps to our advantage Anna had scared Lena Michaels half to death.

Cam and I lunched alone one day. She feigned surprise at Lena's disappearance, particularly since she'd said not one word – just up-sticks and disappeared, kids and all.

She still seemed to consider Lena a friend. However, between practice, rehearsals, touring and being a wife and mother there wasn't time to dwell on other things. Anna was more of a mother to Katy than Cam ever was, and Nik was like Rob – forever taken up with work.

For a little while, things weren't too strange. We were trying hard to keep Rob's life as normal as possible although it was inevitable that sometimes Anna forgot.

Once, she found a frog, bleached and belly-up, floating on top of one of the garden pools. Empathy made her flip it over and poke a finger on it. It promptly jumped from between her fingers and hopped away under a bush. To be fair to her, Anna hadn't known her Dad was watching.

On another occasion, he saw her jump onto a high wall and land on her feet, floating down like a fairy.

There were other happenings but those are the two which immediately come to mind.

On each occasion, looking as if he might vomit and no matter the time of day, Rob left for work where the whole world performed in a predictable manner.

Both Anna and I were so proud of him. Despite the shocks and problems he never once failed in love for us. He stuck with it, sometimes to the point of tears. With her empathetic nature Anna would often sob on his knee.

I thanked God everyday he'd been such a pain in the ass and chased me until I married him.

He was unique and always found a silver lining to every cloud. The one with the frog was, 'Damn but it walks like Charlie Chaplin with the shits." Then he laughed out loud when Anna wrestled him to the floor and pummeled him.

I think his basic problem, understandably, was fear of the unknown. Anna in her no-nonsense manner pointed out he knew Grannie Meg, Momma and me and he wasn't scared of us."

"You think?" he said with a grimace.

It was becoming more and more evident that Anna's gifts were far more all-encompassing than Molly had told me. She'd said she was an Empath – a sympathizer – and a Resurrectionist – raiser of the dead. This was true, but she was also a telekinesist which meant she could move objects by the force of her will, although I have to say for Anna there didn't seem to be much force involved – she just did it. She could also move *herself* which is what Rob probably saw when she floated onto the wall.

Despite nearly strangling Lena Michael's at Cam's house and showing no shock when Molly had shoved Layla over a waterfall, she had not one ounce of badness in her – just a childish impatience with the non-magical world. Molly said she'd grow out of it, but scared the hell out of me when she followed it up with:

"She'll have to. She reaches her majority in eighteen months and that's when her full powers will be revealed."

"You mean there's MORE?" I asked aghast, wondering how I'd explain it to Robbie.

"I don't know. After I'd met the Sisters, there was with me."

Well, thank God for that. I could keep them away from her unless giant monoliths had learned to fly. They were on the other side of the world.

I was very troubled about what the future held for our daughter – well, for all of us really - so I took Rob for a gigantic pizza and an even bigger jug of wine, to share Anna and Molly's horrific news of what was to come. When the time came I chickened out. I couldn't do that to him. More of his normality would be chipped away soon enough.

"Let's do the beach…" I giggled. "I do could…*I could do* with some… air."

"No shit," he said, hefting me by the arm across the road, with a huge grin on his face. I hadn't seen that expression since he was stung by the Sisters. Looked like being an interesting stroll.

I gave him a wobbly smile.

I needed to know more, and as Molly's visits to me were so intermittent, I decided to question Anna. I needed to put her in a good mood first.

The conversation didn't go as I'd intended at all. For a start it was held in front of Rob.

"What would you like to do today – beach, museum or just go shopping in LA?"

"Whatever it is, you might as well ask me now. You don't need to pay me for it. Sorry – that was thoughtless."

She seemed to spend so much of her life apologizing for what she was, I felt almost as sorry for her as I did for Rob.

Chapter Twenty-eight

Light Relief Followed by an Unexpected Realization.

I decided perhaps it would be better to keep the conversation about Anna's future to myself for a bit longer. Rob needed more time to assimilate what he'd been told and Anna needed her self-belief back. It could wait.

So Anna called Katy, and for a change we traveled the short distance to Torrance Beach, which was quieter than Huntington. The day I chose had no concerts – which could be raucous – and the beach, clean and tidy in the morning sunshine, was virtually deserted.

The girls had both taken flying leaps into the water before we'd even unpacked the car trunk. Naturally there was an array of cameras, and a picnic.

Rob set up a volleyball net, and the girls continued batting the ball back and forth long after we got tired.

"Old…I'm old," groaned Rob into his towel. "I might be dead tomorrow. Almost forgot, I've a daughter who can resurrect me."

That thought had not been as cheery as it should have been.

It came to me for the first time - and with a jolt - he wasn't my cheeky Robbie O'Connor any more. He was in his late forties and an overwrought business man, having learned the hard facts that most of his clients were shits, even though the photography fascinated him as much as ever.

Now he was having to cope with the most appalling upheaval of his life.

When we were halfway through our first Margarita pizza, Anna said:

"We haven't seen Grannie and Grandpa for years. Why don't we ask them over? Uncle Joe and Auntie Zella too. It'll be fun for Meggie-Claire and Jack."

"Excellent idea. What do you think, Rob?"

In view of my previous thoughts, I looked at him carefully and saw the tiredness there. Perhaps this wasn't the right time, but he brightened up as I spoke and behaved as in my heart I knew he would.

"Wow, you're a genius. What a magic idea! I'll ring as soon as we get back."

Anna looked at Katy and raised her eyebrows.

He was going to become Anna's version of me and Deidra and find ways of coping by teasing her unmercifully. It seemed it was the O'Connor way of things.

To say he was middle-aged didn't mean he was a has-been. He proved that afternoon he could outswim all of us with ease, even through roughening waves. Only when he could see Katy was struggling did he head for shore and towel himself dry.

"I'll teach you to write me off, Anastasia O'Connor."

Witch Ethereal

"You should give up, old man," said his daughter, "You'll give yourself a heart attack."

In view of what I'd learned over the past few years, I hated it when she said things like that. I didn't trust that she was joking at all.

The following day when Anna and I were alone, I found her in the garden, poking about for dead frogs or fishes to resuscitate in the pond – at least that's what I thought she was doing, since she was elbow deep in water and silt and sinking several water-lilies in the process.

It turned out, in an odd way, I wasn't far off the mark about resuscitation. She looked at me with furrowed brow.

"You remember when <u>Molly</u> told you I was into the big stuff in a couple of years? Well, I'm not ready – nowhere near. I've raised one healthy dead lady, a frog, a racoon and a couple of birds. That's nowhere near good enough for Queen Mab and Jack-in-the-Green!"

"Who the hell are *they*?" I asked distracted, as I assembled a posy of velvet-red roses to put on the hall table.

"I promise never to tell <u>Molly</u> you said that. She'll have you removed from the sisterhood! Queen Mab is in charge of flower spirits and Jack is often called 'The Green Man', but basically he looks after trees and bushes," Then as an afterthought, "Very simply put."

"I thought they were just in children's fairy stories – like I read to you when you were knee high to a grass hopper."

"He keeps an eye on them too – they're mostly green."

Time to move on.

"Do you know what will happen?" I asked her, trying to sound laid-back about a series of events which would throw all our lives into disarray.

"Not really. I have to go back to Westmoreland at some point. <u>Molly</u> was vague about the details. I don't think she knows."

She looked thoughtful for a few minutes then said:

"When I asked her she said it was far above her pay-grade. What does that mean?"

"It means she's not high enough up the chain of command to be told."

"Oh…that doesn't sound hopeful. I rely on her for explanations when I get lost."

"Perhaps as you're due for the 'Big Time' soon she's trying to wean you away from her, so you start thinking for yourself. You do sometimes – you did with Jill. Perhaps that should become second nature."

As she walked off and sat on the grass, deep in thought, Puddy slinked up beside her and stretched, purring, across her legs. A bright blue butterfly alighted amongst her curls and for a moment I was put in mind of my mother and Smyltandale.

I had the strangest, most gifted child in the world, yet my feelings towards her were so conflicted. Of course, I loved her more than my own life, but I was also more than a little frightened of her.

I was putting so much trust in Molly to guide her when I couldn't, that it filled me with apprehension. It sometimes seemed to me Molly's own superior powers made her glib, but she seemed to hold Anna in great respect. This had seemed beyond weird when she was a small child, but now Anna was a young woman I was beginning to see what Molly meant. Her presence had become commanding. I knew she was far beyond my control. Both her father and I would be a part of her life or not, as she chose. Rob would never survive her not wanting him.

Chapter Twenty-nine
Return of the Grahams and Greenwoods

Cam asked if she and Nik could take Anna with them when they went to Lake Arrowhead in the San Bernardino mountains, a couple of hours drive from Reina del Sur. Katy would love to spend time with her, said Cam.

They'd hired a pretty house overlooking the lake which had its own mooring and motorboat.

"I'm sure she'll be thrilled – how kind of you," I said. "I'll get back to you. She's gone to the beach – she'll be here soon."

Rob, of course, thought it was a splendid idea. He had no off-button where his daughter was concerned. He didn't see she might inadvertently kill someone or chuck them over a waterfall.

There was the added advantage of a week on our own with no interference though.

Anna was given the usual lecture from her Dad of 'if you feel witchy sit on your hands', the implication being she needed them to wave her wand. She'd taken to undoing his belt so his pants dropped to his ankles in retaliation, although so far, thank God, in private.

We all knew this joking around was going to come to an end sooner rather than later. No-one said anything, but we were all heartbroken – Anna as well – that her childhood was just about gone, and she had no idea what would replace it.

In the end she went to the Lake with our blessing, and a suitcase full of swimwear and makeup like any normal teenager.

When it came to what her future held, Anna was afraid and excited at the same time, but I was truly terrified. While she was away, I looked for all the information I could find, but naturally the local libraries didn't have sections on 'Witches, Hierarchy and Training of'.

All I could find was a little backstreet shop in LA which had a broomstick stuck to its fascia and baskets of dusty dried herbs. Of note was a box of nutmegs labelled "Bezoar, goats – good against nicotine".

For Robin and I this was a time to rekindle our romance. Our lives seemed to have been fraught for years and we needed alone time terribly.

For three of the days of Anna's absence we only got out of bed when we ran out of energy, needed food or, once, to answer the door to an embarrassed parcel delivery man. We also spent serious hours seeking confidence from each other reflecting on our past and future lives.

I had an awful presentiment Anna would have to leave us sooner or later but could say nothing to my husband until I was sure.

Witch Ethereal

Robbie had never told Dan about the dinner at Cam's and what had happened to Jill, but if he wanted to keep him as a friend, he'd have to. We couldn't risk Anna or Katy letting it slip accidentally.

I had no idea what Cam and Nik thought, but clearly there had been something odd about the happenings at their home, first with Jill and our family locked in a bedroom long enough for the LAPD to turn up, then Lena's peculiar disappearance soon afterwards. It was difficult to know whether Danny would be more upset by knowing or not knowing.

In the end, Molly made the decision for us.

As we lay gasping in each other's arms from yet another bout of delirious lust, I heard the familiar 'pop' and Molly appeared at the side of the bed. I was so shocked I jumped and ended up on the floor.

Robbie's head appeared over the side of the bed with Molly hovering at his shoulder.

"What the fuck! She's not here again? Tell her to bugger off – we can't get it on with her standing by! I thought she only showed up if you let her?"

Molly's face was a picture.

"I used to like it." she said resentfully. " Not with the Graham idiot but I had a nice little number going on in Annan with a chap called Billy Horn – aptly named!"

She hooted with laughter.

"Lord above, I'd forgotten the pleasure until I saw you two puffing and panting. Thanks for that!!"

"Rob's right, <u>Molly</u>. You don't have permission to be here. How did he put it? BUGGER OFF."

Rob was swearing profusely at only being able to hear one side of the conversation.

"Okay – I'll be on my way. I only came to give you a message from my Lady. She says to tell Danny, and Jill – who's Jill?"

"Jill's Dan's fiancé and I'd like to keep her as a friend, if you don't mind."

"Your daughter has more access to knowledge of future events than either of us – never mind Danny and this Jill. Ring your mother like she told you."

Poof! She was gone.

Rob had given up. He'd showered and was in the process of dressing by the time <u>Molly</u> had finished her instructions.

"She says we've to tell Danny and Jill something, and I've to call my mother and invite the family over for a holiday."

"I'm not saying a word to Dan," he said, viciously pulling on his socks. "Anna can do it. She'll know what she's talking about. Ring your mother."

That's how four days later, as Anna returned from Arrow Lake with Cam – the Greenwood and Graham families, minus Jack and my father, arrived at Reina del Sur.

Jack was with a true love he was joined at the hip to I was told with affectionate laughter.

Predictably, Dad wouldn't let anyone else shoulder the responsibility of his animals, so despite our mutual affection, he was still at home in Scarsdale. Perhaps I'd go with Anna.

I was shocked by my mother's appearance, but then it had been years since I'd seen her. She was just the same but the lines on her face had deepened and her skin, rather than tanned as it usually had been, was now ruddy.

Uncle Joe was still as brown as a berry, with those far-seeing eyes peculiar to men of the hills and vales of Westmoreland. He had lost most of his fine white hair and put on a pound or two round the middle, which suited him.

Zella was – well, Zella. She hadn't changed a bit apart from her accent which had acquire the broad vowels of the north of England. She was so excited to see me she was lost for words, so she hugged the breath out of me instead.

Hanging shyly back in the doorway was Meggie-Claire. She was a stunning beauty with her mother's piercingly intelligent turquoise eyes, and her Dad's hair, thick and pale as it had been in his youth.

"She prefers to be called Greta," said Zella, looking pained, "she's extracted that from Margaret."

"I think that's very pretty," I said, "Grown women can't be called Meggie-Claire."

Greta smiled with such warmth she reminded me of Rob.

What had surprised me the most was that I hadn't accounted for the passage of time.

Greta must have been in her early twenties, which made Mum and Uncle Joe in their late sixties, and my Dad in his seventies since he was four years older than Uncle Joe. I saw my mother glance sideways at me on a number of occasions and I could see she was thinking the same. My appearance wasn't so markedly different because I'd become a city girl, and my clothes were fashionable and my hair, still long, had been straightened and finely cut.

After I'd made tea from the several pounds they'd brought over because they thought I'd be missing it, we sat around chewing the fat for an hour or so. They passed on news of the farms and fells. I told them about Rob and his studios, and the success he'd made of them.

They all still thought of our daughter as Anastasia until I reminded them Mum had recommended we shorten her name to Anna when she was just weeks old, so we had.

As they were all exhausted, I showed them to their rooms to clean up and rest. Greta stayed and sparkled at me for another half-hour until she too, could keep her eyes open no longer.

Witch Ethereal

She was a real beauty, and pleasingly naïve from her country upbringing. She reminded me of me, before Rob and I moved away, only I wasn't so beautiful. If she batted those long pale lashes so reminiscent of her mother's at any of the LA males, they'd fall at her feet.

When they'd all disappeared to rest, Anna came breezing in from her holiday, with Katy and her parents in tow.

"Are they here yet?" she said, looking about her.

"They are, but tired from the journey so resting."

"Good. I need to see Greta," said Anna, ignoring any empathy which might have been forthcoming in an Empath.

No-one else noticed, but I was puzzled that she needed to see someone she didn't know, and that her name was Greta. When she'd seen her last she'd been Meggie-Claire. The news came from <u>Molly</u>, I supposed.

"They've brought me huge amounts of tea from England. Like a cup?" I asked Nik and Cam.

"Iced please, with lemon," said Cam and I was profoundly grateful Rob's mother wasn't there. She'd been fazed by coffee for breakfast when we'd stayed at Nik's chalet on Huntington Beach. Putting ice and lemon in tea would have given her the vapors and Cam severe earache.

"I'll have some too," said Anna, "but first I have to speak to Katy about Greta. We'll be in the garden."

Cam and Nik stayed to chat about their holiday waiting for Anna and Katy to finish their time together in the garden,

After an hour or so, during which time the girls hadn't reappeared, I repaired to the kitchen to plate up some snacks and replenish the tea. As I filled the microwave jug, I happened to glance out of the window.

Anna, Katy and Greta were sitting in the shade of a California palm at the edge of the lawn. I wasn't entirely surprised that Greta was no longer sleeping, since her bedroom opened onto the garden and had sliding doors. I imagined Anna had woken her.

Katy and Greta were listening in fascination to what Anna was saying. The eye-contact was intense.

I'd stopped what I was doing to watch them when my mother, refreshed from her nap, came to help with the tea.

"She's putting together her Coven – don't forget Greta also carries the blood." said Mum following my line of sight.

I looked at her in surprise.

"Molly paid me only her third visit in my lifetime, so what I am telling you she must have thought vitally important. She said Anna would probably need our help. You know Greta's related to us? Robert Graham was my father and Joe, her Dad, was the result of Claire's affair with him."

It had never entered my head but it was true – she was part of the Carrick-Graham direct female line, like Mum and me.

"Grandad Greenwood told me the Graham cycle in England was complete and my fate was here in California. He told me there would be nothing left for me in Westmoreland. He didn't tell me my daughter could be Glinda of the North – well at least I hope she would – she might turn out to be the Wicked Witch of the West. She's bossy enough."

I could feel myself getting more and more pessimistic as the thought developed.

"Have you retained you powers here?" asked Mum.

"Except for Molly, no. But she pops up everywhere – mostly unexpected and usually at the most inappropriate moments. Anna can hear her in her head but unfortunately I have the doubtful pleasure of seeing and hearing her as clearly as ever. She calls Anna 'the Lady' and says she's Wicca royalty. The problem is, I believe she's probably right."

At that moment Joe, still slightly damp from the shower, and smelling strongly of aftershave, came to ask where the hell his tea was. That put an abrupt stop to the conversation until he left.

"Oh, please let me tell him," gasped my mother. "Not only does his loony sister think she's a witch, but his daughter does too."

As we finished the tea, each of us broke into the occasional giggle at her own private thoughts.

Witch Ethereal

Chapter Thirty

Getting to Know Each Other Again

The three girls had become close and got on really well. There was a difference in their ages but it hadn't seemed to matter.

They spent a lot of time at Reina del Sur, and went swimming, failed dismally at surfing and went to a beach disco. I had the feeling though, much of their time was spent in what I can only describe as 'business meetings'. I tried once or twice to listen in but they shut up like clams when anyone else was near.

Naturally Zella was keen to see Nik again.

The meeting took place a week or so after my family's arrival, at the Chilton's beach house.

Zella proudly introduced her daughter and we all laughed at Nik's immediate response to her beauty:

"Can she sing?"

"Not a note," said her Dad hopefully, managing to look nervous and confident at the same time.

Greta gave her father an affectionate shove.

"I did a bit at school but that's all."

There were kisses and handshakes all round. Zella only knew Cam vaguely from when she visited Nik at his office, but both seemed to get on well. Zella's confidence had improved since she'd married a multi-millionaire, although her charm had remained.

Robin kissed the hands of all the ladies and winked at Greta who blushed. Anna groaned.

Zella promised to drop in again to see Nik and Cam before they left, as they air-kissed their goodbyes.

Two days before our family's departure, Anna had taken me by the hand and walked me to the little summerhouse in the garden so we could talk privately.

"Greta needs to come back on her own."

No 'by your leave'- I wondered if she'd even consulted Greta.

"I was rather expecting that. Apart from me and Grannie Meg, she's the only other female blood relative. Has she shown any abilities?"

"She's a bit vague about it. She seems to be in tune with nature but I'm not sure how. You know – like Grannie's good with birds and butterflies. Greta seems to understand animals and flowers…and things."

She looked puzzled. She clearly hadn't given it much thought.

"I suppose she must know Jack – not that one, Jack-in-the Green."

If I ever knew what she was talking about, I'd forgotten.

While we're on the subject, do you have any ideas about <u>Molly</u>? She seems to do as she likes – she flits about all over the place."

"She was head of the Dumfries Coven. Her powers absorbed those belonging to the rest of her sisters."

Wasn't that a turn up for the books? I didn't know, but it did answer a lot of questions. It answered, for example, how Robbie and Joe had been able to sense <u>Claire</u>, and I could see her even though she wasn't a relative. It also explained how <u>Molly</u> was hanging around Reina del Sur, half a world away.

"We're getting off the point. When can Greta come?"

"Anytime she likes. She can stay behind now if it's okay with her parents. We'll take her home again when they want."

"Good. Tell them she'll be home after my birthday. You know why – Grannie Meg told you in the kitchen."

Another bloody guessing game – my life was wall to wall papered with them. Was I supposed to remember every word of every conversation?

"I need her here," she said decisively, brooking no further discussion.

"Of course she can stay. Need? Is that the right word?"

"Yes," Anna said, picked up Puddy and went to her room.

So it had turned out to be a waiting game again with Anna in charge.

"We can't stretch this out any longer, Robbie," I said, sad that he looked so tired. "Whose it to be – Dan and Jill about the broken neck or Nik and Cam about the same and Lena's disappearance"?

Chapter Thirty-one
Danny and Jill Confront Anna

Rob and I decided it would be better to face two likely disasters one at a time, and Danny and Jill drew the short straw.

He also decided the best place for Anna to tell them about the happenings at Cam and Nik's, would be to buy ribs and fries from a take-out on the ocean front and eat them at a picnic table by the beach. Anna loved them but I hated the scrape of grit on my teeth when airborne sand hit sticky sauce. Still, if that's what it took to get us through this ordeal, so be it.

Dan and Jill arrived, Dan dapper as ever in tailored shirt and pants, beard neatly barbered. Jill, not quite Greta's equal in the looks department, nevertheless looked chic and sophisticated.

Anna and I arranged the food on the table, her mouth sucking on rib before I'd managed to spread everything within reach of everyone else. I stared a reprimand at her which she ignored completely. She took another one and slathered it in barbeque sauce. I hoped she wasn't going to be difficult. Afterall, the trip to England was her 'coming out' so to speak and this would be the first time her abilities were given a public airing, I assumed in preparation for events to come.

I began to small talk and when that ran out, thoroughly exasperated at the nervous looks around the picnic table, Anna huffed:

"Oh for Christ sake, Mother, there's no gentle way of breaking this," then turning to Dan and Jill she said emphatically:

"I'm a high-ranking witch."

To prove it, one of the spent ribs from her paper plate hovered over her Dad's head for a few seconds before being deposited in a trashcan several yards away.

Dan shot to his feet in disbelief.

"How'd you do that? Do it again!"

One of the little feral cats, which sometimes darted along the sea front, shot into the air as she remotely tweaked its tail.

"Sit down. Dan," said Rob with trepidation, "That's not even a party trick. We have something to tell the both of you, which I hope and pray you're not going to hate us for. We are telling you these things from love. Hold that thought. Anna, take over."

"Jill, do you remember the night of Cam's dinner when you fell over and choked and Dad laid you on a bed to recover? Do you remember Momma had called me to come over?"

Jill nodded wondering where this could be leading.

"You died and I healed you."

Dan leapt to his feet, and he landed my husband a left to the jaw which almost certainly would have felled an ox.

I raised a groggy Robin to his feet and he gingerly massaged his face.

Meanwhile, Dan had begun to run off down the promenade, I supposed before he could do any more damage to his friend.

"STOP!" ordered Anna.

Jill looked from Anna to Dan and back again, but before she could move, Dan had drawn up rigid as if he'd run into a brick wall.

He looked back at Anna, mystified, then tried with more force to barge his way through. Anna's mouth compressed slightly but that was all. Dan tried to move to one side, then the other. Anna's right index finger twitched. She wasn't even trying.

In the end Dan was obliged, sweating with fury, to return.

Jill did her best to calm him, but now he wasn't just offended, he was terrified. I felt so sorry for him.

"Don't be afraid," I said, "We've grown up with this and we're still here. So is Jill. Anna always works for the good, unless someone is trying to hurt her loved ones – then she defends them with all her might…which is considerable.

"The tassels on Jill's shawl got wrapped round the carved back of her chair and when it tipped over throwing her on the floor, she choked…… then her neck snapped. We all heard it."

"We took her to a bedroom and locked the door," Anna continued, her empathetic nature fighting its way to the fore. "Dad laid her on the bed, I felt for the break and prayed hard for it to heal. I had help though – from half a dozen other witches who'd crossed the Veil.

"The WHAT?" said Dan, doing his best to keep up.

"Don't try explaining that Anna, it'll take too long," said my whey-faced hubby, rubbing his hands wearily over his face.

"Here, Anna," I said, handing her a ten dollar bill. "Wine won't cover this - go and buy a bottle of anything intensely alcoholic from any liquor store."

"I'll go," said Rob, relieved to find an excuse to get away, "She's a kid - they won't serve her."

He jogged off across the park.

"Take a hike, Anna," I said, before she could say *something* to offend *somebody*.

Jill was looking at me, hands clasped tightly on the table top.

"It's true, isn't it?" she whispered.

I was taken aback by her easy acceptance, and took a few moments to collect myself before I replied:

"Ghastly as it may seem, yes it is."

Dan was shaking his head from side to side, unable to believe what he was hearing.

"When I was laying on the bed, before I woke, I saw some old women standing with Anna. They were only shadows. I did see them, but only for a split second. I thought I'd imagined them, that it was part of the unconsciousness before I came to."

I wasn't about to make matters worse by asking if one of them had long curls and a white skirt. <u>Molly</u> was sure to have been one of them.

"Please don't. Don't tell me all this abracadabra stuff makes sense to you – that a sixteen year old girl is capable of raising the dead."

"You'll be pleased to know, Jill. You hold the honor of being the first human she's experimented on. Anna was the only chance you had for survival. The best she'd done, before you, was a raccoon at LA Zoo. She was about as scared as she's capable of."

Jill looked startled, Dan sick.

"And what's Rob's take on this?" asked Dan, "Do Nik and Cam know about it, or Rick – he's into the Third Dimension stuff?"

"Same take as ours, I guess" I replied, "seeing as he was present when Anna was doing her thing. It may be of comfort to know he looked as bad as you do now the entire time.

"He'd already seen her raise birds and resuscitate dead plants but preferred not to notice. The gifts only run down the female line so you're in good company with the men of my family. They're as blind as bats and deaf as posts as well."

There were a few moments silence while Dan thought that through.

"I don't feel well," he said. "I think we'd better go home, Jill. I've to fly out tomorrow. I'll come see you Monday."

Chapter Thirty-two

Proper Magic

We collected Anna and returned home.

"Well, do we tackle Cam and Nik or aren't you up to it yet?" I asked Robbie who sat with me drinking the strongest whisky he could find for Dan.

"Would you be particularly upset if I jumped off the Colorado Street Bridge? It's not far from the Pasadena studio. I could get there in ten minutes," Rob muttered.

"I wouldn't if I were you," said Anna blithely, standing behind him and kissing his ear. "You might spend eternity with Layla – Millard Falls is only twenty miles away. She knows you and it's relatively local."

He put his elbows on his knees and head in his hands.

"I've tried to understand – I really have - but I just can't," he said through bitter tears.

Anna knelt between his knees, taking his head on her shoulder, and comforting him like a child.

"Would you do *anything* to make this sadness go away?" she asked.

"Anything," he mumbled into her neck.

"I love you Dad. I wouldn't do anything to you without your permission. You have to agree. If you do, I can show you why I am as I am. If I'm right, you'll understand."

"Could you be wrong?"

"Not likely," she replied, with confidence.

In our room, Rob lay down on the bed. The trust in his eyes as he looked up at his daughter was wonderful to see.

Anna put out her hand and gently covered his eyelids, holding them shut with the lightest of touches. When she removed it, Rob was deeply sleeping, his long eyelashes fluttering occasionally, as if he was dreaming.

She looked down at him with more love than I had ever seen her express for anyone, then turned to me and grinned:

"He'll be out for at least a couple of hours. Let's go for pizza.

"What? You're going to sit and look at his immobile body for two hours? You can't influence what's happening to him. That's why I asked his permission. He's visiting the people he knows beyond the Veil in dreams."

"That'll be his mother and father – oh God! – and <u>Molly</u> and……<u>Claire</u>. You'll never wake him."

"Don't be silly. You've never been able to get rid of him. Why would he change that now?"

We did a bit of grocery shopping then slid into the banquette seats at Anna's favorite pizza parlor in Huntington. Half way through our pepperoni, Anna suddenly sat bolt-upright, her eyes wide.

"Go home…go home now and sit with Dad. He shouldn't be alone when he wakes up. I have something to do."

With that she fled, leaving me stunned and still with a mouth full of pizza, staring after her.

The sun streaming through the doors, cast lights from Anna's amber hair making it spangle as it streamed behind her.

She excused herself as she almost knocked over two teenagers in the doorway. They appeared to know her, but she was gone before they could speak, leaving them, like me, open-mouthed.

I saw Anna holding out her hand in the familiar stop sign I'd first seen when she was a baby rescuing a frightened kitten.

She wove her way between the cars and cabs, and reaching the sidewalk, pelted towards the pier.

I was panic-stricken. She'd told me to go home, and I knew I should – Rob might need me. I looked at my watch. I'd a little more than an hour left. Shuffling along the seat I dashed after her, dumping the pizza box in a trashcan near the door.

Anna had reached the pier – I was just in time to see her skid round the corner. I stopped, gasping to get my breath back – she was a teenager, I wasn't.

On the pier surely she had to slow down but I saw her running its length, legs pounding, hair flying.

At the end of the pier was a covered tower which housed a coast-guard station and had a small coffee bar. A platform which served as an observation point was built out on pilings over the sea. As usual the walkway was laden with tourists, families with children, fishermen with baskets and rods in canvas hold-alls, teenagers holding hands and laughing in the sunshine. It was a scene of happiness and contentment. What on earth had spooked my daughter, who was still running full pelt, towards the end of the pier?

As Anna neared the end and I was half way along, I heard a creak and a groan as the struts beneath the platform began, one by one, to give way. Before anyone could do anything the walkway tipped violently sideways and people were trying desperately to cling to its boards.

My daughter took a flying leap which lifted her high into the air and dived down to the foaming waves beneath.

The first of the holiday-makers, mostly children as they were the lightest, had begun to hit the water and a dreadful screaming began.

The platform hadn't yet separated from the pier but the groaning, rasping noise increased until eventually the whole thing ended up on its side in the surf.

Anna was treading water just feet away and I saw her stretch out her hand and turn it in a circular motion. The platform flicked over on its back and became a raft. She swam over and began dumping children onto the boards, every so often flicking her wrist and heaving half a dozen more into the air by magic. Such was the panic, no-one seemed to notice.

The coast-guard had launched a boat to pick up any remaining people from the sea.

Anna hauled a man onto the platform and was giving him CPR, but I saw her look surreptitiously around and place her palm on his chest. He coughed, spluttered and pushed her away, breathing hard.

I wondered what happened to people when they first passed over. This man's behavior, like Jill's, didn't seem to indicate they'd reached the Veil.

Anna looked straight at me and motioned me toward the beach, beginning to swim to the shallows.

She took a few seconds to get her breath, then seized me by the hand and ran me to my car.

"Get going," she huffed, "unless you want Dad to have a heart-attack when he comes to to an empty house. He's likely to be a bit overwrought."

She opened the window and spat out a lungful of sea water.

"Anyway, we've to get out of here before I'm front page news in the national press."

"You couldn't have expected anything different."

"Shucks," said Anna, totally unimpressed.

Chapter Thirty-three
Robbie On-Side (at Long Last)

Once home we went to check on Rob. He was still snoring peacefully. In fact, I hadn't seen him look so peaceful in an age. He was smiling slightly, as he had been laying outside Nik's beach house, fast asleep with his camera propped on his chest as when we first visited America.

"Come on, Grace Darling. Let's get you dried off and into some fresh clothes," I said, hugging and kissing my brave and beautiful daughter on the cheek.

I sat on the bed while she dressed and dried off her hair.

"What do we do about Dad?" I asked.

"Nothing I shouldn't think. He'll be so annoyingly full of the joys of Spring, he probably wouldn't notice we were there."

She continued to brush out her long tresses.

"What's that in your hair?" I said, leaning over and taking a strand between my fingers.

It looked a bit like the multi-colored holographic sprinkles put on children's cakes. I checked it out closer. As I tried to stroke it with my finger, it disappeared only to reappear on another part of her hair, where it turned blue.

"What is it?"

She shrugged and continued to slide the brush through her curls.

"It's only magic. It's not there all the time – just when I've used rather a lot in one go. That's what's left over. It'll disappear in a minute or two."

Puddy twisted round Anna's ankles, looking up at her and purring loudly.

"She loves magic," said Anna.

"Where the hell is everybody!" yelled a panic-stricken voice. "It's gone from bedlam to total silence in seconds. What happened?"

We raced each other to the bedroom and got briefly stuck in the doorway before Anna popped through first.

"We were rather hoping you'd tell us that," she said.

He lay back on the pillows and his face was filled with a radiance I'd never seen before. It was as if he was lit from within. He was distracted for a moment and peered at Anna.

"What've you got in your hair?"

He pulled it down for a closer look and the sparkles disappeared.

"Never mind that!" she said testily, "How did it go?"

"I *saw* everyone – EVERYONE - but for your grandads, Angela.

"Hardly a surprise," Anna chuckled.

"My mother told me to go away and not come back until I popped my clogs – it was like the old days! Dad grinned and I noticed he wasn't wearing his boots. Ma's prayers answered.

"<u>Claire</u> was there. She kissed me – and I felt it. She gave me a ten shilling note and said there was a John Wayne film on at the Roxy in Nethershaw.

"It was odd, they didn't seem able to gauge how old I was. It was as if I was still ten."

"Those are the times they remember you with the purest love," smiled Anna, "It would be different for each of them."

Robbie scrabbled about in his pocket.

"<u>Claire</u> tucked the coin in here."

His hand came out empty.

"The dead have no need of money. It was a kindness she conjured up to make you happy – as the real one used to do." I explained.

He looked disappointed but said:

"Now I understand how you felt, Sweetheart, when I couldn't…wouldn't believe you about seeing <u>Claire</u> – or any of them, come to that. He kissed me softly on the lips.

"Did you dream <u>Molly</u>?" Anna broke in.

"Did I dream <u>Molly</u>? God, yes! She could talk the hind leg off a donkey. Between calling you 'My Lady' and 'Your Highness', she told me all about you. She also told me things I'd to swear not to pass on, even to you – especially to you."

Anna opened her mouth to protest but Rob held up his hand to silence her.

"One thing I *can* tell you is if you continue to wheedle, all the good you've done will be undone. Don't."

Anna wasn't used to being thwarted and I could see it didn't sit well with her, but if <u>Molly</u> had said it, she didn't doubt its truth.

"Give some thought about what reversing today's happenings would mean, Anna," I warned.

She bit her lip and nodded seriously, although her brow creased, and I saw a brief glimmer of the graveyard eyes she'd flashed at Rob and me at the Sisters when we were being obstreperous.

For the very first time I saw the aristocrat in her. It wasn't lost on Rob either. As he was about to lift her in his arms and swing her round, as he'd done since she was a toddler, he stopped in mid-movement and rubbed his cheek tenderly against her hand, then kissed its back reverently.

"You don't need to do that Daddy – ever. Of all the creatures on earth and out of it, you will never need to do that. I will never love anyone as much as I love you."

She turned to me adding, "He understands, can't you feel it?"

For a moment there was a tiny glimmer in her hair but it was gone in a heartbeat.

"And you will always be my Momma. You are my strength, you put me right when I veer off-track."

"Are you so taken up with the other side of the Veil you've forgotten to ask Anna about today?" I smiled at Rob.

Anna recounted the afternoon's happenings with an odd mixture of humility and authority. Humble bossiness sounds a contradiction in terms but with our daughter, it wasn't.

When she'd finished I felt as if I'd stopped breathing.

"Stop it, you idiot," said Anna, "Not breathing is a bad idea for anyone this side."

I realized I must have gone pale and my knees were wobbly.

Robin cuddled me on the bed. When the color returned to my cheeks he asked Anna:

"How many did you pull out of the water."

"Twenty or thirty, I guess."

I was dumbstruck and I'd been there. I replayed the happenings in my mind.

"But I saw fifteen at most!"

"It must have been about twenty-five then. You can't have seen the ones floating under the pier. That's where I dragged the dead man from, but the others were okay."

"Dead man? What dead man?" I asked.

"I found him banging about between the pilings beneath the pier. He'd taken a crack to the head and was floating upside down. I got the rest out first then went back for him. He'd not been gone long. He came back pretty quickly."

"Molly's right, isn't she? About what's to come when you're eighteen," said Rob.

"Yes," Anna confirmed.

She sat with a thump on the bottom of the bed.

"What's today's date?"

"June 21st," said Robbie, "Why?"

"It's precisely two months to my eighteenth birthday and I'm not ready. I'M NOWHERE NEAR READY!"

Oh God, was time really so short? Molly had said she'd come into her full powers when she was eighteen. After what I'd seen that afternoon, I couldn't imagine what the rest of them might be.

Chapter Thirty-four
Cam and Nik, Danny and Jill

Once Rob had stopped floating on air and looking starstruck, I made us pasta and I tried my best to have some kind of ordinary people-type conversation – not an easy thing with a witch and a born-again believer, but I tried my best.

I couldn't say the same for the other two. They looked set on downing my culinary effort as quickly as possible to get back to the matter in hand.

In the end I gave up and we took our wine to the living room to talk.

"Before anything else," said Rob, making a determined effort to be sensible when all he wanted was to dance round the room, "we've to sort out the problem of our friends.

"Jeez, I hope they're really good friends or we're going to be relegated to the funny farm. Perhaps if they all came at the same time they could support each other in their disbelief."

He examined his finger nails so he didn't have to look us in the eye.

I'd had similar thoughts and wondered if Anna had any useful suggestions to make.

"Can't you have a chat to Theia, Anna?"

"I already did. Yesterday. She says there are too many variables. Usually seeing the future is easy for her, but the mix of dead and non-dead people means there are so many unknown elements. Add magic to the mix and she can't be sure of anything. But Molly says to get the hell on with it - I'm needed at the Sisters."

Anna dashed off a call to Greta. She demanded a meeting at Reina del Sur before they both returned to Westmoreland, so it had to be now.

Rob deferred a meeting with Alan and Steve who were travelling to Santa Monica and made the phone calls himself – first to Dan, then Nik and Cam. At Anna's insistence, they were to bring Katy with them – another 'business meeting' for the girls, I supposed.

Nik and Cam were delighted to accept the invitation. When we told them Dan and Jill would be there too, they were thrilled – it was rare we were all together. Rob and I suggested we might take them out for dinner later in the evening. I just hoped and prayed they had some appetite left when we were through.

We were dreading it - except Anna who seemed if anything, relieved. This two months to D-Day situation was really playing on her mind. She was putting all her confidence in help from Molly. Having had past experience of that lady's unreliability, I feared for Anna. It was clear this was going to happen on August 21st with or without Molly's assistance.

Witch Ethereal

I helped Cam off with her coat, while Rob slapped Nik on the back with more than usual gusto. Nik gave him a sideways glance, alerted immediately to the suspicion this might be a little more than a social occasion.

Anna grabbed Katy's hand and dragged her to her room where the record deck, turned to full volume, would hide any conversation.

Dan and Jill had already arrived, Jill sitting demurely on the couch and Dan, running his hand repeatedly through his hair, was pacing the room. He ended up sitting on one of the chairs at the patio table, so the others joined him there.

A few minutes later Rob and I arrived toting a tray of various alcohols and a bucket of ice, hoping it wasn't going to be needed too badly.

As each chose their drinks, and ice tinkled against glass, Cam opened the conversation, smiling uneasily, having picked up on the mood of the other guests.

"So who's murdered who?"

Dan, dropping ice into his brimming glass of Scotch said:

"Oh, it's a sight worse than that! Get Anna down here Rob. She needs to explain this herself. God knows, nobody else can."

He swirled the ice round in his glass and dashed the lot off in one swig. I refilled it for him.

<u>Molly</u> was standing behind Dan's shoulder smirking.

"Best of luck. There might be a few more residents this side of the Veil before the day's out," she chuckled.

I came within a whisker of telling her what I thought of her, but just in time controlled my face and kept my mouth shut.

Rob didn't need to find Anna because at that moment the two girls strolled down the stairs and helped themselves to Colas from the fridge, laughing and chatting.

Dan leapt from his chair red-faced and resumed his pacing dangerously close to the pool's edge. I just prayed Anna would resist the temptation of giving him a mental shove.

"<u>Molly</u>," said Anna, to explain her own and her friend's sudden appearances.

"Who the fuck is <u>Molly</u>?" said Dan.

"Don't swear in front of the girls, Dan," warned Cam.

"Don't swear? Oh boy, are you in for a shock!" he replied.

Jill said quietly:

"Sit down, Danny. You're not helping the situation. I'll try to explain what I know myself because it involves me directly. You too Cam and Nik, although you won't realize it."

She told them what had happened at the dinner party.

Dan, who had experience of Anna's powers, looked as if he might burst into tears. Nik was speechless.

Rob refilled the glasses. Katy laughed at something Anna whispered in her ear.

Finally Nik managed to say:

"She's a sixteen year old kid. You have to be joking."

"She's seventeen and in two months she'll be eighteen," I said.

"Is that significant?" asked Cam, marring her perfect features with a frown.

Rob, afraid he might have to explain how he was involved in this situation, had been doing his best to keep out of the way. Besides which, he was still most inappropriately cheerful, but he thought I needed some moral support so said:

"When Anna turns eighteen she becomes independent and will be a full-blown Coven witch."

Nik dropped his glass. It smashed on the tiled floor and shattered.

He summoned his poor daughter who had never seen her father as angry as this in her entire life. When she hesitated, Anna gave her a push.

"Yes, Papa?"

"Have the whole O'Connor family brainwashed you?"

"No, Papa. I've always known. Ever since the first day I met Mrs. O'Connor. Even before I met Anna, I knew."

"How?" asked Cam, mystified.

"Anna can speak in my head if she chooses, like Molly speaks in hers."

"Who the hell is this Molly?" demanded Dan again.

"She's Angie's great grandmother. She died in 1937. She's Anna's mentor on the other side of the Veil," said Rob, in a futile attempt to explain.

By this time Dan was pretty much speechless, so his part in the conversation was minimal. He stood, hands in his pockets, grey-blue eyes tense with concentration as he tried to make sense of matters totally beyond his comprehension.

"What *is* the Veil?" asked Jill, picking up on the most important point, "You mentioned it before, Angie."

"Don't. Anna – don't even try to explain that. They're spooked enough," I warned.

Nik wasn't to be distracted. He continued grilling his poor daughter who was quailing before his anger.

"Hearing voices in your head? Isn't that schizophrenia, Cam? Is our daughter deranged?"

"Oh for God's sake" said Anna, and raised the table, contents and all, four feet off the ground, disturbing Puddy who had been fast asleep beneath. She returned it carefully to its previous position.

"I'm getting a bit fed up with all this party trick stuff. I'm a witch – not a bloody conjurer."

I sometimes wondered where Molly got the empathy thing from. I could only pray our daughter's temperament would improve in August.

"Do to Nik what you did to me," instructed Dan, "Nik, go stand on the path and try walking towards the gate."

As before, and while Nik was still walking away, he stopped dead, then pushed and shoved at the invisible barrier, trying to batter his way through it. This time Anna had done the job properly - Nik was imprisoned.

With a twitch of her finger she released him and he walked back to the table appalled.

"Okay, okay," said Dan, "That's one thing, but raising the dead's another. What happened to Jill's different."

I saw Anna raise her hand and her hair glittered with spangles. No-one had seen her hair glimmer with magic except me.

"No, Anna!" Rob yelled in terror, afraid she was going to do to one of our friends what she'd done to the tiny bird she'd resuscitated as a child. For once, she did as she was told.

We sat silent and sipped our drinks.

The light was gradually fading and the smell of jasmine pervaded the air. Fireflies glimmered like magical sparkles amongst the roses. Somewhere a single cricket began to chirrup.

"I'm to be in Anna's Coven," said a small voice, and Katy's father fell off his chair.

"We'll call you in the morning," whispered Cam over the resultant cacophony.

Chapter Thirty-five

Revelation from Cam

Our friends left thankfully still our friends, but Dan made it quite clear there was much more to be said.

In the meantime, Anna had been on the phone to Greta, who knew nothing of the Sisters, which was hardly surprising given that Joe was her father and Zella not Wicca.

Greta and Anna had become good friends which I was very pleased about. Anna had had such a turbulent life, friendship was a difficult concept for her to understand.

Katy was her only enduring friend, and as I had just learned, a prospective member of Anna's Coven. I wondered how that could be, since she had no witch blood. Perhaps Anna could be to her what Molly had been to Claire. It appeared to me Anna could do pretty much what she liked – except see Molly. Whatever the case I'd no doubt Nik would be giving Katy another good talking to before I saw them again.

Anna picked Greta up from the airport. Rather than come straight home they stopped off to eat – to chat privately I supposed. I wondered if Anna wanted to find out the level of Greta's capabilities before she confirmed her in her Coven.

Over breakfast the next morning when Greta was thoroughly rested, Rob said:

"Why don't you find a couple of guys and go clubbing in LA. You don't get out enough Anna, and now your cousin's here it would be a great idea to show her the town."

Greta looked quite keen on the idea but Anna simply muttered:

"Don't know two. If one's okay the other's a troll."

So that was that.

As expected Cam rang next morning and asked if she and Jill could come over the following afternoon.

I agreed but looked forward to it like toothache. It put me in a foul temper which poor Robbie got the brunt of. Loving as ever, after I'd thrown a mega-tantrum, he said.
" Got that off your chest? Let's go to the movies."

We did – "Ghost Busters" – which under the circumstances was about as inappropriate as he could get. Of course, Rob thought it hilarious and sang "Who ya gonna call…" at the top of his voice in the car all the way home.

As intended, he lifted my spirits to the sky, especially when he insisted on smooching on the doorstep like the teenager he still was in his head.

When he came up for breath, I looked up at him and thought he must have a picture hidden away in the attic. He never looked a day older – no, that wasn't true.

He was maturing like fine wine – hair streaked with silver, smooth skin kissed by the California sun, and so tall and slim. But best of all, he love me and our daughter with all his heart and soul. I was instantly ashamed of my bad moods.

Anna opened the door unexpectedly, Greta standing behind her. Rob had to grab the handle to stop falling on his ass. Whereas Greta smiled affectionately, our daughter huffed.

"Goddamn. Grow up! You're not sixteen!"

To which Rob replied:

"Neither are you, Meemaw," and pushed his way into the house with another chorus of 'Ghost Busters'.

Wicca royalty she might be, but she'd never get the measure of her Dad.

Cam and Katy arrived with Jill just before three o'clock. I must have looked like I felt because they grinned.

"Okay, relax," said Cam. "It's not going to be a rerun of the other day. I have something to say you might find interesting."

We sat on the patio with coffee and cookies and Cam began.

"I'm mixed race as you've probably already deduced – my mother was of Egyptian descent and my father a Scotsman.

"My upbringing was confusing to say the least. My Dad had been brought up in a staunchly Catholic family. He was the black sheep – he'd never been religious.

"My mother's family observed Mohammedan rites but their roots went much further back. She always said her line extended back to ancient Egypt where the females of the family served in the Temple of Wadjet at Pe-Dep, not too far from Alexandria. The goddess has many attributes but mostly of protection and unification. It's so far back I can't imagine how she knew the ancient connection was true, but she'd have staked her life on it, so nobody ever questioned her.

"I only mention religion because it's important to our situation. Regardless of the opinion of the rest of the family, my mother's sister – my aunt Halima – was a firm believer in, and practitioner of 'heka', which was a form of witchcraft widespread in ancient Egypt – the word itself means 'magic'. Unfortunately it had, and still has, a bad reputation, much like that of early medieval witches.

"Halima had three daughters who also became adepts, but only one of them concerns us, my cousin Talibah – she's the only one other than me who came to America. We might be able to call on her for backup if we need assistance.

"Do you think I could have a glass of water? All this talking is making my throat dry," Cam finished faintly.

"I'll make some more coffee. Excuse me," I said.

Well, wasn't that a surprise? I wondered what Anna would make of it. She probably knew at least some of it already, if not all, from Katy.

Jill came into the kitchen to help me, and said:

"I'm a bit player in this, but I wanted you to know I believe what you and the girls are saying. Things did happen to me when I was…er…deceased… and only now are they coming back. I really don't know what to make of it. Mostly there are two faces – both are vague as if viewed through a fine mist."

"A veil?" I asked.

"Yes – that's it exactly. Through a veil. How did you know?"

"What did these people look like – what you could see of them?"

"One was a woman with a strikingly sweet expression – it seemed to be her defining feature."

"Blonde hair, slim?"

"Yes. Did you know her?"

"She sounds like my Uncle Joe's mother, Claire Graham. And the other?"

"The other was a man – tallish."

She stopped to think, frowning.

"There was something unusual about his appearance, his complexion. He waved to me through the…veil. It was very odd."

"<u>Josh Greenwood</u> – my grandfather - he froze to death in a storm before I was born. I used to see….."

I chuckled.

"Both of them are…were lovely."

"How did you know who I meant? I couldn't give you anything but the vaguest description."

"Just lucky guesses, I suppose."

"The veil was as insubstantial as mist between us. I walked forward to speak to the figures but couldn't get through. It looked like a haze but felt rigid.

"Then there was a jolt like an electric shock and I was sitting on the bed next to Rob. I promptly forgot the whole thing. It's been coming back to me in dribs and drabs though."

I thought of <u>Molly</u>'s description of the Veil being like mist but stronger than steel.

Anna strolled onto the lawn from the French windows in Greta's bedroom. From the kitchen we couldn't help but hear her loudly announced to no-one in particular:

"My mother sees dead people – not many, only family and close friends – but those she does see are clear and very chatty."

It was perhaps for the best that Cam wordlessly interrupted Jill and me. She joined us in the kitchen, picked up the tray and carried it back to the patio, where we sat for a few minutes sipping our espressos.

Katy's sensibilities, not helped by the dressing down from her father, were a little less forceful than my daughter's. She appeared out of fresh air at her mother's side:

"Tell Mrs. O'Connor the rest, Mama. It's important she knows," she said, before running off into the garden to be with Anna.

"Katy's abilities are subtle, as you've just seen," said Cam, "She can move without being seen. She's a quiet person anyway as you know, but when she's in company, it can be uncanny.

"I try to discourage her from listening to other people's conversations, but it's not always easy when they don't know she's there.

"She can also see magic. That's how she became so attached to Anna. She told me when they first met she was spangled all over with stars. I'd never heard of that before."

We decided to call it a day and take some time to think things through, but one thing was clear as day to me - although Anna had never mentioned it:

Her Coven was slowly coming together.

She was right – time was short.

Chapter Thirty-six
Over to You, Jill

I walked my friends down to their cars and Jill asked:

"Does Rob believe you both, or is it only us girls?"

Cam took one of her fancy cigarettes from its gold case and leaned against her car hood.

"He does believe it…now." I said, "but it took a long time – like thirty years or so. In the end, Anna bludgeoned him into it by reconnecting him with his deceased mother who threatened him with hell and damnation if he showed up on the other side of the Veil before his due time."

They began to laugh.

"Don't laugh - you didn't know his mother. She'd scare the crap out of you. Deidra and Robbie locked horns until the day she died. Thanks to his daughter, Rob's since found out she probably hasn't finished with him yet."

"Poor thing," chuckled Jill who hadn't quite got the idea.

"He fought Deidra all his life but there was a bond between them few understood. Since she left he's had no-one to grapple with, and there's a huge hole in his life he can never fill. When she died he was heartbroken.

"Danny and Nik both met her – did you know? Deidra pretty much adopted Dan at a time I think he needed it most. She took a swipe at my husband who was looking Danny up and down with a camera to his eye. She clipped him round the ear for being rude – he was about thirty at the time.

"<u>Deidra</u>'d have sorted this God-Almighty mess in five minutes flat by telling everyone what their opinion was, then making them do what she said."

My eyes filled with tears.

"Oh Lord, I miss her."

"Do you suppose Anna'll sort Nik and Dan out too?" asked Cam, cynically, "if we ask nicely?"

"I don't think so. She'd probably advise them to 'get real'. She only took Rob on because it was that or a shot gun. He was driving her up the wall."

"So what's next?" asked Jill.

"I honestly don't know," I said, raising my shoulders. "The three girls seem to have things pretty much under control.

"I forgot to tell you, Cam. Anna says she and Greta will be going back to England soon. She'd like to take Katy if that's okay – or to put it in Anna-speak 'We're going to Scarsdale and Katy has to be there too'."

"I can tell you now Nik won't allow it."

"Then we'd better fix up another meeting and change his mind. I know you'll be inclined to take his side Cam, but in this case I'd advise against it.

"Greta will go home to her parents but Katy and Anna can stay with my mother. You'll appreciate all this is something Mum knows about. She has powers too although she's not what you'd call accomplished. She and Deidra thought me seeing dead people was hysterical."

"Dead people!" Jill whispered then louder – much louder, "DEAD PEOPLE?"

"In Egypt, I do too," said Cam. "Only our Veil is called the Tet of Aset – the Knot of Isis, to give her her Greek name."

It was my turn to be gobsmacked.

"You do?"

"Yes, but they're tied to a location and I can only see people close to me, although I occasionally see vague shades of others."

I ran back into the house and brought out a full bottle of wine and three glasses. They could do as they pleased but I needed this.

"That's precisely like me!" I said, "I don't see anyone here because all mine are in England. Except for Molly, that is. I haven't figured out my great grandmother Molly Carrick Graham's place in all this yet – but I will.

"The oddest thing of all for me, is that Anna is virtually all-powerful, but she can only hear Molly – she can't see her. And Deidra won't show herself to Anna because she says doing so would – and I quote – 'scare the crap out of Robbie'. She might change her mind about that now, I suppose, since he knows something of what's happening – even if he doesn't exactly understand it."

"I'm doing my best to keep up," said a flummoxed Jill, "but I have no connections so can only follow every other sentence. Whatever you say I have to go along with since I've been on the receiving end and my memories are becoming clearer. But it seems to me, the major problem we have now is getting all this through to Dan and Nik. Do you think they'd believe Rob?"

"Doubt it. Nobody ever believes a word he says – he spends too much time winding people up.

"Anna's given the pair of them a demonstration, but apparently they thought she was a stage magician with tricks up her sleeve."

"We'll just have to keep trying until we find a way to get through to them," said Cam.

A voice from the steps interrupted us.

"Just make sure you're at Scarsdale for my birthday. Greta, Katy and I are booked on a flight already. I'll expect you at Smyltandale a few days before the 21st. Uncle Joe and Grandpa will be a nightmare. You'll be needed."

"Cam was just saying she didn't think Katy's Dad would let her go."

"I think you'll find he will."

She hooted with laughter and flounced back into the house slamming the door behind her.

My two friends were shocked.

"That's nothing unusual," I said by way of reassurance. "She's been like that from birth. It's never directly affected you before."

"Katy's always known she wasn't like the other kids," said Cam. "How about Greta?"

"Thanks to my Uncle Joe – her Dad - Greta's never discussed her abilities with anyone. I suspect that's the reason for this visit before they all have to go to England."

Chapter Thirty-seven

Where's Robin O'Connor (Again)

It was the beginning of August – just three weeks before D-Day – when Rob went missing.

The three girls were in LA buying final items for their journey, so I decided to go to the studio in Santa Monica where Rob had meetings and take him to lunch.

The receptionist brought me coffee, and I sat in Rob's office, leafing disinterestedly through his in-tray.

There was a polite knock at the door. Don, Rob's studio manager, poked his head in and said:

"Hi, Mrs. O'Connor – looking good!"

He always had that 'cheery chappy' thing about him. I waved him in.

"Bring me a coffee, Cath," he shouted through the open door, "Like another?"

I shook my head.

"It's nearly two-thirty. He shouldn't be long – he has a guy coming in to see him in about half an hour. Mind if I get on? I've a pile of work to do. Just yell if you need anything."

He left, taking his coffee from Cathleen's hands as he went.

I waited and waited. No Rob.

Witch Ethereal

He wasn't the most punctual person in the world so, although I was irritated, I wasn't alarmed.

By three-thirty, that had changed. I began to feel uneasy.

Then all hell was let loose.

Anna came flying through the door, hair streaming and eyes wide.

"Where is he? Where's Dad?"

I was frozen to the spot. Anna NEVER panicked. When the whole world fell to bits, Anna stood in the middle of the carnage and began to pick up the pieces. A quick image of her in the bistro and the smashed glass and wine flashed through my brain.

"Where is he? Find him NOW?"

I shoved a gawping Don and his secretary out of the door, shut and locked it and tried to calm my daughter but she was frantic.

"Deep breaths, Anna – slow down. I can't help because I can't understand you. Now…what the…"

"Molly," she panted. "Molly spoke to me. "She said…"

"Just hold on a minute. I'll get you a ch……"

"I've no time to wait for goddamn chairs – Molly said……"

"There's no need to be ru……" I said, offended.

"There's every goddamn need! <u>Molly</u>'s exact words were: 'Get that poisonous woman away from Robin or you'll all, him included, be sorry. If I could get my hands on her I'd rip her to pieces, but it'll have to be you over there, since I don't have hands - to speak of - on your side'."

"What the hell does that mean? That's gibberish, even for <u>Molly</u>."

"Oh, God, Mother! Stop being so obtuse!"

I was so busy trying to calm her down I wasn't paying a great deal of attention to her words.

The outside door banged shut.

"There you are. Don said he was due back. He's got a meeting."

Anna was out of the door like a rocket, but it was only Rob's three o'clock appointment who'd arrived late.

"Did you hear from him?" asked Don round the door in whispered anxiety, "This is an important guy and I can't sign the check."

"Here, I'll sign it. How much?"

I took Rob's briefcase from the desk drawer and made out the check.

Don grabbed it and disappeared again sweating, and pasted on his best placatory smile as he left.

"I wouldn't worry too much, Honey." I said, stroking her hair, "Your party trick is resuscitating frogs – his is doing disappearing acts."

She was crying and shaking her head.

"<u>Molly</u> wouldn't say something like that without good reason. She loves us."

I couldn't think of anyone who might be described as poisonous. My acquaintance was limited – my family and friends were all in England except for Jill and Dan and Nick and Cam.

Jill was too pleasant to be thought of as poisonous and Cam's friends appeared to be the same. Cam was of the blood herself, as was Katy. But apparently <u>Molly</u> assumed it was someone we knew.

"I want to go home Momma," said Anna tearfully, "and I want you to come with me. Greta can go home with Katy."

"Hadn't you better call Cam first. She might have something else on."

"No, she hasn't. Get your jacket."

Chapter Thirty-eight
A Disappearing Act

Anna dropped Katy off at Cam's door then drove us home at Rob-style speed.

She sat on the couch, curls for once wild and unbrushed. It was clear she was petrified and didn't know what to do.

"I'm sure he's alright," I said. "You know Dad. He'll turn up."

"That's just it. He would never worry me like this."

"He's done it to me – twice."

"But that was different. He doesn't have any reason this time and…….did you get a warning from Molly?"

It was true I didn't. My warnings generally came from Grandad Greenwood. Molly was wise and full of springtime joy, but there was a nagging thought always at the back of my mind she had her own agenda.

"Go and see if any of Dad's cameras and lenses are gone. That might give us some idea where he went. He wouldn't take a wide angle lens to a studio or a portrait lens to take shots of the ocean."

We couldn't find his big expensive Nikon but all the lenses appeared to be in place. It could well have been at any of the studios.

Rob's managers couldn't help. Rob always locked his precious cameras away so they weren't sure if anything was gone or not.

"Try calling <u>Molly</u> up again and see if she knows anything else."

"I did. I got the 'search your heart, it'll come to you' shit."

"This is wasting time. We have nothing solid to go on. We don't know Dad's missing and hasn't just gone on a jaunt of his own devising – wouldn't be the first time.

"Then we'll have to get off our butts and go look. It's better than just sitting here."

Neither of us had a clue where to begin, so after a brief discussion we decided to check out places he liked to spend alone time.

We walked Torrance, Manhattan and Redondo Beaches where he loved to take his camera, but the Ocean walks and sands were teeming with people. We drove up to Santa Monica – even as far as the amusements at Palisades Park where I'd found him when his mother was dying.

We drove through the mountains, an hour and a half, all the way to the house at Santa Barbara, now in the hands of a letting agent. It was unoccupied, the garden sprinklers turned off, the grass parched.

We could think of nowhere else, so as it was now dark, we went home, thinking Robbie might be there.

He wasn't.

Anna was frantic. Apparently, Molly kept dinning in her ear we should hurry up – not only for Rob's sake but time was getting short for the three girls to be at Scarsdale, and Dad or no Dad, she had to be there.

Between us we tore the rest of Rob's home studio apart. Anna had already been through the closet containing his cameras and lenses. Now, we went through drawers of old shots, photographic paper, pegs, string, protective gloves. His three guillotines were propped haphazardly against the wall.

Under the sink were his developing chemicals. I dragged Anna away before she hurt herself.

When we'd finished the place looked as if a bomb had hit it. He'd better have a damn good reason for being away or, if he wasn't dead already, he was about to be - if he didn't strangle the pair of us first for trashing his inner sanctum.

Neither of us slept more than ten minutes at a time so by daybreak we were off again, hyped up on coffee and doughnuts.

We combed the beaches again, now quiet. No sign.

"Let's check out the studios again. Al or Steve might have thought of something else. He might have had to go off unexpectedly for work."

"They've got bloody telephones," I grumbled.

"He might have called when we were out. We left at just gone three and didn't get back until nearly midnight."

Alan sat on the corner of Rob's desk at Serenity Studios, thoughtfully stroking his chin.

"We haven't seen him since last week. You've been most places I'd have thought of. Anything been troubling him lately?

Anna and I exchanged a meaningful glance. We'd thought we'd put his mind at ease. Perhaps not.

Al picked up Rob's desk diary.

"What's today's date? August 3rd? Wasn't it about now there was the incident with Layla at Millard Falls?"

"No," said Anna rubbing her forehead. "It was August 2nd."

No doubt <u>Molly</u> was yelling in her ear – it would account for the sudden headache she seemed to have developed.

"He was devastated by that – you could be right… Let's give it a shot – come on."

"Let's go, then," said Al, jingling his car keys and diving out of the back door into the very same alley Layla had run down to her doom.

We bolted up the mountain-side, vaulting the narrow streams. At the top all three of us stood with our hands over our ears against the deafening roar of the waterfall.

Alan leant over the cliff side as far as he dared, but saw nothing, so we split up and searched across the turf and between the trees – still nothing. My mood hovered between relief and disappointment.

On our way back, I crossed to the broad pool at the base of the waterfall in case he'd fallen straight down, but he hadn't and I could see no trace of him where we'd found Layla, lodged on the shelves of rock above.

I shook my head at the enquiring look from the other two as I stepped back onto the path.

"Come and eat," said Alan, "while we try to figure out where else to look. I've a map in the car and there's a take-out at the Visitors' Centre."

We examined the map chewing disconsolately on pepperoni pizza but came to no conclusions.

Al called Steve at Huntington to ask if he had any ideas.

"He went down to Dana Point last week to suss out some locations – that might be worth looking at. There are some great coastal and ocean shots from there. Then there's the harbor, and a bit inland is Capistrano. Lots of meat there for a photographer. Ever heard him mention it?"

I looked at Anna and we both shook our heads.

"Never," I said. "I've never been there, but it doesn't mean he hasn't – he goes lots of places I don't know. If he had a commission for a vacation company or the State Tourist Agency, do you think it's the kind of place he would choose?"

"Very likely," said Alan, rubbing his hands through thinning hair.

Anna was massaging her forehead and had her eyes closed.

"We may as well take a look," I said. "If we don't find him I'll call the LAPD. There won't be any other option."

I cursed him under my breath. God help him if he wandered in smiling, and wondering what all the panic was about.

We piled into my car and headed south past windswept beaches until we reached the flowery meadows above the Point.

Anna opened pained eyes and I saw a glitter of violet spangles spark across her hair, quickly gone. She must have been grilling <u>Molly</u> - bit of a shouting match by the looks of things.

Dana Point is such a beautiful place for nature lovers. Remote from the Babylon which is Los Angeles, Californian poppies like golden sovereigns are flung across fields which drop precipitously to pounding surf. To one side is a narrow beach of coarse sand, and to the other a mixture of smooth and jaggéd rocks, heaped or spread in a jumble of grey, blue and sand.

We followed the cliff-top trail south towards the harbor, leaning over the cliff to scour the melée of stone and surf at its base.

"There!" shouted Anna, "What's that over there?"

Before I could even move she was climbing hand over hand straight down the sandstone slope, kicking footholds in the crumbling rock as she went.

When she got to the bottom she turned to her right and clambered over the uneven shore until she reached a shallow depression between the stones. Something lay in it, but I couldn't see what it was from so far away. Then I realized Molly was standing next to me, impatiently tapping her foot. I glared at her then realized Al must have thought I was looking at him, since he was standing on her other side.

"It's a…... Looks like ……but …... There's no …… ……soaked through."

Her words were whipped away by gusts and the roar of surf.

"She says the bag looks like her Dad's but there's no camera and everything's wet," translated Molly.

"Thanks Molly."

It was said disparagingly and I was immediately grateful when another blast took my words away too.

"What's that?" said Al.

"Oh, nothing. Just wondering what Anna said."

There was a path no more than a foot wide running at a steep angle down the cliff.

Al stayed behind as I hurried down it as quickly as I dared. Molly was there before me, standing at the foot of the cliff still tapping her foot.

I was out of Anna's line of sight but Molly was mediator.

Apparently, Anna'd found a plain white handkerchief lodged under a stone. Rob carried one sometimes to clean his lenses but it was unremarkable and could have been from anywhere.

As I hurried towards my daughter, my ankle buckled on the uneven rocks and I fell, twisting my wrist and bruising my shoulder and cheek. I couldn't stop if there was the remotest chance this concerned Robin. I hoisted myself to my feet and limped on, flinching with the pain.

To my left, along the shore line, black holes appeared, gradually increasing in size from rabbit-holes to caverns.

Finally, I grabbed onto Anna's arm and managed to gasp:

"We've to get up top NOW. The tide's coming in. We'll drown."

"You go. I'll stay till I've found him. I can feel he's here, I can feel him."

A sheet of pink and gold sparks flashed over and between her darkened curls and picked out her features. The glow turned silver, then menacing pewter as she raised her head and examined the cliff above.

Looking straight down perhaps fifty feet, from the top of the cliff, was a woman's figure, a silhouette against an ever darkening sky. A gale whipped the skirt round her legs and snapped at her hair.

The roar of the waves took on an ominous tone, the surf crashed, the wind howled.

I glanced at Anna, who had turned all her attention to listening to <u>Molly</u>.

As in all similar situations when the actions of the dead might affect the fate of the living, no help could be expected from beyond the Veil. The living had to make their own way, rise or fall by their own experience.

"You must leave, Momma. Between us <u>Molly</u> and I can manage. I can feel he's here somewhere. Go on and don't worry. I can hold back the water long enough to be safe."

She pushed me back the way I'd come, then when I resisted, her brow furrowed and I could see she was losing patience.

"I can't do this if I've to worry about both of you."

The path was steep and tough-going with a sprained wrist and twisted ankle, so I'd to force my way onwards.

By the time I reached the top I was weeping with pain. I'd stumbled more than once against the gravel path and one of my knees was grazed and bloody.

Witch Ethereal

Finding out if Al had seen the mystery woman on the cliff top became my objective, since her appearance had made Anna frighteningly angry.

Al took in my tattered appearance and ran to bring the car round. I yelled against the storm:

"I can't leave. Anna's still down there and the tide's coming in. She believes she may have found Rob's camera and refuses to come back until she finds him. She's convinced he's there somewhere."

This would have been more believable had he been able to speak to Molly or observe Anna's star-spangled hair.

Al moved to climb down the path to the shore, but stinging needles of rain had begun to blow in our faces and were making the muddy path slippery.

"Don't Al," I screamed. "You can't do anything. Perhaps she'll find rocks to climb on out of the way.

Even if this was the case it was likely the ocean would whip her away. Unless she could call on her magic…and Molly.

Witch Ethereal

Chapter Thirty-nine

Grief

"How long does it take for the tide to go out again?"

"I don't know," replied Alan, "Several hours I would guess. There are caves along the cliff there – some quite big. If she could get inside one of those and climb as high as possible she might be okay."

"Did you see the woman on the cliff top when Anna and I were on the shore? She was standing just about there."

I pointed.

"No, I doubt I would have in any case. All my attention was fixed on you. What did she look like?"

"I couldn't tell – she was silhouetted against the sky. All I could make out was that she was slim and had hair long enough to blow in the wind."

As it was going to be a couple of hours wait at the very least until we could climb down again, there was nothing for it but to sit in the car out of the wind.

The storm was slowly abating and my attention was fixed on the cliff top, but still I saw nothing.

At one point, <u>Molly</u> popped up beside the open car window.

"I shouldn't be telling you this, but one and a half of them are okay."

Witch Ethereal

She faded from sight.

What the hell did that mean? Half was missing? Which half of which one? I stood there wishing she'd bugger off and stop leaving me with half-clues. I also wished that Al could see her then I wouldn't have to maintain this ridiculous charade. I was already stressed enough.

Unless Anna came back there wasn't a lot of point in getting out of the car again. The shoreline was pitch black so I wouldn't be able to see a thing. I watched the rain drops chase each other down the windscreen.

Al had fallen asleep and was snoring gently. I wondered if he'd a wife to go home to, and if he had, if she was wondering where he was.

By the time I could resume my search it must have been near enough five o'clock. The sky had begun to lighten but remained still starry from the fading night.

The sea was now still and the waves lapped softly against a rock-strewn shore, swilling peacefully into hollows and depressions.

The graze on my knee had scabbed over and the blood on my forehead dried, although my wrist still hurt like hell and was twice its usual size.

I'd no time to dwell on that. All I could think about was Molly's 'one and a half'.

Finally, I found Anna sitting on a rock gazing out to sea and looking thoroughly exhausted. She was star-spangled from head to foot, although it had become muted, and as I watched, faded away altogether.

Alone on the seashore sat an ordinary exhausted teenager. I held her to me, petrified of what she had to say.

Of all the inappropriate things, Molly was jumping up and down with glee.

"Told you – one and a half. Well, it's two now!"

She turned and skipped into a large black opening in the cliff face behind us.

"Some leader *you'll* make!" she hollered over her shoulder at my poor Anna, who was doing her best to struggle to her feet, still ashen-faced.

As I followed Molly through the cave entrance, a tall ghostly figure stood against the wall – Rob, looking worse than I'd ever seen him.

His knees buckled, and he fell to the floor.

"Please can we go home?" he begged.

I realized we weren't alone in the cave although Rob didn't know, couldn't see. Molly stood beside the entrance and ranged around the perimeter of the circular cavern were seven other women.

I could see them quite distinctly. They were of different ages and different styles of dress. All stood to attention like soldiers on parade.

Witch Ethereal

"Why are their eyes still shut," I asked Molly, "The rest of them seems pretty normal apart from being green."

"They only open them occasionally when there's something they consider worthwhile. I've never seen them do it myself."

One of the figures was considerably taller than the others, and wore a linen bonnet tied under her chin and a long ticking skirt and cotton apron. She looked as if so inclined, she could flatten Sonny Liston.

Molly dragged me forwards by the arm until we both stood before her.

"You always wondered about the Sisters – well, here they are. This delicate one is Maggie McGowan, of my direct line – eight or nine generations past. You can see there's little resemblance."

She was right. Delicate joyful Molly bore no resemblance to this scary vision.

But then a remarkable thing happened.

Maggie, eyes still firmly closed, smiled and the entire cave reverberated with the sweetest humming – like the Sisters I knew, but ethereal, almost fairy-like.

Molly walked round the other six, introducing them one by one, finishing with the last, a young girl of about Anna's age with an aura of bashfulness about her. With each introduction, the humming increased in volume. It was effervescent and made me feel I was about to take flight.

My attention was briefly drawn to a puckered scar across the youngster's neck and she, eyes still tightly closed, pulled her shawl tight to her chin.

"This little one is Jeannie Thompson. She was garroted with wire before she was burned, which is why she carries the scar.

"Believe it or not she and Maggie are the oldest here. They were amongst the Dumfries witches strangled and burned on White Sands in 1659. Jeannie's still a bit nervous.

I supposed she would be, having been strangled and burnt, but it was over three hundred years back, so perhaps it was time she bucked up a bit.

Her tentative smile put me in mind of Katy Chilton.

I was distracted by a loud groan from behind me and suddenly remembered my husband looked – pardon me – like death warmed up.

Anna flopped down beside her father and rubbed his arms to get the blood flowing. He was trembling all over.

"He's shattered, Momma. He hasn't a clue what's going on. We both keep talking to Molly and the Girls. Being resurrected is pretty exhausting – we should get him home. Is Al still up top?"

"RESURRECTED?"

But for that one word, not another was forthcoming.

"Yep. What do you these are all are doing here? I suppose I'll be able to raise the dead on my own eventually, but for now I need a bit of extra power to my elbow."

I looked down at Rob who was decidedly the worse for wear.

"Home," he croaked desperately.

'The Girls' – straight faced – turned to mist and faded into the cavern walls.

"See? Understand the one and a half now? He was still coughing up the Pacific Ocean when I left and part of him was behind the Veil, but he'll be alright now.

Chapter Forty

The Strangest Conversation

I thought once Al had dropped us at home, Rob would go to bed to recover and we'd speak when he'd rested, but he seemed too terrified to close his eyes.

I suppose if you took a peek behind the Veil, being able to open your eyes becomes a major consideration.

Not so Anna, who took herself off to bed at the double.

I took the quilt off our bed, wrapped him in it and propped him up with pillows.

He still had a yellowish tinge about him although his color had begun to return.

"Do you feel like explaining? Might help to get it off your chest, don't you think?"

"Lena…she threw my bag over the cliff and I watched my Nikon shatter against the rocks."

As an afterthought he added:

"She shoved me after it."

I was appalled. What possible reason could she have for doing something so cruel? Surely it had nothing to do with the school incident years ago, or Anna nearly strangling her with her scarf at Cam's dinner party. Why pick on Rob? Of the three of us he was the least guilty of any wrong-doing.

"I got washed into the cave you found me in. The water carried me higher and higher until I was lodged against the roof and I began to choke. That's all I remember. The water must have receded quite quickly because when I opened my eyes Anna was there, kneeling next to me with her hands laid flat on my chest. They were really hot, searing – I'd to push her away."

He'd no clue what had happened. This meeting with the mystical wasn't such a joyful occurrence – he hadn't been given a brief reassuring glimpse in a dream, he really had crossed the Veil. He'd been dead for some time.

"I must have been dreaming again – or perhaps my brain was starved of oxygen…

"I saw my mother – how come when I've done something stupid she's always the one who turns up? She said. 'I told thee before to sod off home. Tha's no business over here. Now get lost and look to yer own concerns. Yon lass'll burn a hole in tha chest. Get going.'

"My Dad was standing behind her laughing his head off, like in the old days. Then I thought my chest had exploded – there was this terrific shock like lightning and Ma and Dad had gone. I was frozen stiff, wet through and staring up Anna's nose. She burned me – look."

He pulled back the quilt. Naturally, there wasn't a mark on him any more than there'd been a scar on Jill's neck.

It was now my turn for an explanation. What he was having to accept was getting more and more bizarre.

"You were dead – that's why your mother yelled at you to get back. Anna returned you to us like Jill, and as she did with the bird when she was trying to explain how our gifts worked, and you needed an illustration."

Robin still wouldn't sleep so I turned on the TV and cuddled him like a fractious child. Eventually in the comfort of my arms, his eyes fluttered shut.

As I was lounging on the couch with my arm gradually going numb from the weight of his head on my shoulder, I got to musing on how we were to get Dan and Nik on a plane to England.

I didn't suppose Cam would have any more luck with Nik than I would have had with Robbie before his epiphany. She could always use the promise of a free holiday as a lever I supposed and keep the threat of taking Katy without him as a clincher.

And Jill? At least Nik was rational. Danny seemed to have lost it completely. Jill may need some help.

The absurdity of it all suddenly struck me and I laughed out loud, thereby jolting my poor husband awake.

Once he'd ascertained he was still in the land of the living, he softly snored his way back to oblivion.

I'd pretty much got it right.

Witch Ethereal

Cam used Katy as a lever to control Nik – and with great aplomb, I had to admit. She insisted as her mother she was just as fit to keep her eye on Katy. While not wholly convinced, Nik finally agreed.

It was a little more difficult for Jill. Firstly, she was a diffident kind of person, not used to shouting the odds. The exact antithesis of Dan in fact.

She did have one ace up her sleeve, though, I hadn't anticipated. She sent her engagement ring back with a note which read.

"If you are so ashamed of me you can't introduce me to your English friends, I see no hope for our future."

Ooph! One up to Jill.

Even though the note was rubbish, as anyone with half a brain could have figured, it had been one hell of a risk to take with someone of Dan's temperament.

"So what happens now?" Jill asked Cam and me as we sat in a smart little downtown bistro in LA.

These little afternoon jaunts had become a regular and enjoyable feature of each of our lives since the dinner party.

"The three girls seem to have their own tickets. So we'll need some for us," said Cam, looking dubious. "That's a bit of a tall order in such a short time. I'll get on it right away when I get home if that's okay."

"Sure thing," I said, fishing the pineapple out of my Mai Tai.

It'd become abundantly clear we were all thoroughly bored with the whole topic, and Jill was beginning to think there was a definite case for calling off her engagement permanently.

The whereabouts of our little tête-à-têtes was well known to our girls, so it didn't come as a surprise when following a deal of giggling at the door, in waltzed Greta – old enough to be there; Anna – not old enough to be there; and Katy definitely not old enough to be there.

Cam jumped to her feet on the point of roaring at her daughter. I dragged her back into her seat.

"Don't bother. The barman won't even notice," I said.

"No," Cam conceded. "He won't have seen Katy either. Speaking of which…where is she?"

"Gone to powder her nose," said Anna laconically, and Greta giggled and added:

"She's leaning on the bar."

"I saw Lena today."

Anna dropped this bomb-shell as she leaned over and helped herself to the prawn I'd just peeled. She was so blasé at first I missed her meaning.

"She was at the 'swap and meet' in Huntington. I got this. Do you like it?"

She whipped a wad of tied-dyed Indian fabric from a bag tatty from overuse.

"It's ghastly – put it away before somebody sees it."

"If you go for the hippie look," grinned Jill, "I've a closet full of things that'll fit you. Come over to see me and I'll fit you out. Put that thing in the trash before it infects half of LA."

"Get back to it, Anna. What happened when Lena saw you?"

"Nothing. She didn't see me at first. Katy blanked us out – did you know she could do that Cam? She can shield other people from being seen as well as herself."

I could see Cam, hadn't known.

"Lena…Anna – stay on track. LENA."

"What the hell's Lena to do with anything?" asked Cam.

There was a pregnant pause. Eventually Anna said:

"She broke Dad's camera and pushed him off a cliff at Dana Point. She killed him – I'd to fetch him back. I'd help from Molly and the Girls though."

Cam was uncomprehending, Jill thunderstruck.

"The Girls?" Cam murmured faintly, "Lena did what? *My* Lena?"

"They're…"

"Not now, Anna. Let's stick to the point. What was Lena doing at a flea market?"

"I don't know why she went, but I know why she left. I hit her in the face with a brass pan from the same stall I bought that from. She landed flat on her ass. She was screaming - I made sure she saw me."

Even I, who knew her so well, was flabbergasted by the venom in Anna's voice.

"Didn't you know Lena was a hostile – an ill-wisher?" I said, doing my best to explain to Cam and Jill why Anna had done what she'd done.

"Rob was her second murder. She killed Jill at your dinner party, Cam. Anna brought her back. You must have guessed."

Jill confirmed what I said with a brief nod.

"Oh, God…part of my coming to America in the first place was to get away from all this. It's following me around!"

"You and me, both," I said ruefully, "but if you'd seen Rob after we'd got him home you'd understand why Anna did what she did, even if you don't condone it. It was as if he'd been tainted by the Veil somehow. It took time for him to get back to himself again."

Chapter Forty-one

The Tickets

As promised, Cam rang the airport as soon as she returned home. She'd been fortunate to get cancellations on August 17th. The next available seats to London were a week later, which would be far too late.

"Dan and Nik can please themselves but I have to have you and Dad there – and Cam, Katy, Greta and Jill. It's imperative," Anna screeched.

"You and the other two are fine – you've already got your tickets," I said to mollify her. "Why are you so wound up about it?"

"Nothing to do with you," she snapped, and stalked away.

Molly yelled in my ear:

"She's right. Let her be. It'll all become clear."

"What'll become clear?"

"Search your heart – you know the answer."

For those two I'd light the pyre myself.

Pretty much needless to say, someone took sick on Anna's flight – so Cam and Katy, Anna and Greta where able to leave together on the 13th. Rob, Jill and

I four days later on the 17th so three of our tickets were cancelled – Nik, Dan and now Katy's.

I think, secretly, both Danny and Nik were relieved not to be coming with us. Both were hovering between believing their better halves and the overwhelming evidence, and taking Uncle Joe's view point of complete denial.

We'd a week left to complete our preparations.

The girls and Cam left on the 13th as planned and Mum picked them up.

She took Greta back to Bythwaite where Zella insisted the other three stay as well, but Anna wanted to go back to Scarsdale and stay at Smyltandale Cottage.

I think my mother was a bit put out Anna hadn't chosen to stay with her and Dad at Scarsdale, but she understood she was a teenager, and was agreeable to the idea that they were sometimes a mystery to the rest of humanity – like Robbie at the same age.

I privately thought Anna had planned it that way, as there were things to do before what I'd come to think of as her inauguration. She could hardly speak privately to <u>Molly</u> in a room full of the uninitiated.

I was glad of the few days breathing space. Rob was still looking frail and the separation from his beloved child, if only for a few days, was an added strain.

He had no inclination whatever to be comforted, but I insisted on being outstandingly understanding so eventually he gave in. He'd yet to make me laugh so there was a way to go but I was confident.

"Come on, babe…let's go dancing!" I said.

"Sure."

He hid behind the pages of his Photographic Weekly and paid no attention.

I grabbed the magazine, flung it across the room, jumped on his knee and began kissing him ardently.

He tried to push me away but I persisted, and eventually he responded. His arousal was rapid and all-consuming – and liberating.

There was no dancing done that evening, but a whole lot of love given and taken until the early hours.

"You know, that's our third…" he counted on his fingers, "No… fourth death, and you've rescued me every time. You are the love of my life. I couldn't exist without you."

Tears of emotion rolled down his face and this time comfort was taken in earnest.

That was the beginning of his sure recovery. In the small hours, we laughed intimately and made silly whispered small-talk.

"I wouldn't let the Veil separate us," I whispered, knowing full well the choice wasn't mine.

Given the mood of our last parting, Rob thought it might be kind to invite Danny and Nik to nearby

'Charcoal Joe's' restaurant and treat them to a juicy prime rib.

He didn't say so but I guessed the general idea was to try to reassure them we weren't as crazy as they thought we were. He gloomily reminded me of the day by the river at Ghyll Howe, when he'd first learned I could see <u>Claire</u> and <u>Molly</u> and had been so furious with me. Now he was in the same boat, his courage was failing fast. There was every possibility he was about to lose the best friends he had in the world.

What could I say? He was probably right.

Chapter Forty-two

Danny, Nik and a Whole New World

For once, Dan wasn't somewhere else so we agreed to meet the following evening.

We sat at the bar waiting for them, then ordered our food and beer and sat at one of the semi-circular tables which lined the walls.

Nobody spoke. It was awful.

We'd no idea how to open a conversation about the supernatural which half the company thought, if not ridiculous, then surely impossible.

It was true they'd experience of Anna's abilities, but the only example they knew of her true power was what happened to Jill, and there were ways they could twist that into disbelief like my Dad did.

In the end, it was Rob who broke the ice.

"Did you hear from Cam and Katy, Nik? Anna's at Smyltandale, the cottage near her grandparents' farm. Angela always refused to have a phone there so I've no way of keeping up with the news other than through Meg and Guy."

"If she's at Smyltandale it'll be because she needs seclusion," I said.

"Cam called last night from Bythwaite. Things Kate says to her, she's finding confusing."

I assumed he didn't know about his wife's proclivities. It was surely out of the question he could live with two witches and not know. Wasn't it? Perhaps not.

Finally, friendship prevailed and we slipped back into easy camaraderie, chattering and laughing, careful to steer clear of contentious subjects.

'Charcoal Joe' Steak Bar is typical of its type in the United States.

A bar ran the full length of a large room. The mahogany counter was polished to within an inch of its life, and shelf after pristine shelf of bottles of every beer and liquor known to man lined the walls, floor to ceiling. Rows of glasses of all shapes and sizes were arranged at hand-height and beneath the bar.

If the Gods on Mount Olympos could have devised a barbeque if wouldn't have matched the aroma – the sheer sizzle – of the 'Charcoal Joe' kitchens.

The only fly in the ointment was a huge oil painting of the city itself which took up most of one wall and was in desperate need of a good clean.

We were halfway through our meal when Dan, with his napkin tucked in to protect the front of his expensive shirt, suddenly said:

"There's a woman over there who keeps trying to attract your attention Angie. She keeps pointing at you and waving."

I hadn't been looking at the room and it was difficult to see clearly through the haze of cigarette smoke, but then...

"Out Rob...out! NOW!"

The others dropped their knives and forks in amazement but such was the force of my order, no-one thought to contradict me.

We collected our belongings and fled, only pausing once we were out on the sidewalk.

My dinner ended up in a conveniently situated trashcan, and I didn't notice we'd been followed outside by...Lena. She'd the remains of a black eye gradually turning into an interesting mixture of yellow and purple. My daughter, I assumed.

The closest person to her was the last out – Nik.

She grabbed his arm and smiled up into his face.

"Hello. I never thanked you for that wonderful dinner your wife cooked for us. How kind! She's not with you I see..."

She looked exaggeratedly about her although it was blatantly obvious that Cam was nowhere to be seen.

"And you..." she reached for Dan but Rob whipped him away from her touch before he could be harmed. What would happen to Nik we'd no way of knowing.

That was as far as she got before she ever so slowly raised into the air, spun gracefully round and smashed face first into the wall behind her.

"There," said my transparent daughter, as she ran an invisible hand down Nik's arm the evil harridan had touched. "That should fix that for now. I'll see to her properly later. 'night Mom – see you soon."

"We have to go home, Rob, fast before we get pulled in by the Feds."

As Rob and I took to our heels, I turned to see Danny and Nik still looking down at the prone body of Lena Michaels, still out cold with blood spirting from her nose. Could it be she'd rammed her own face against the wall? What other explanation *could* there be, they were thinking.

"MOVE!" I yelled over my shoulder.

Galvanized into action, all four of us ran hell bent for leather the four streets to Reina del Sur.

I ordered Nik and Danny to sit down at our dining room table, fetched a large decanter of Scotch and whisky glasses and Rob and I joined them.

"Right. I'm not about to beat about the bush with this any longer. I've had a lifetime of dealing with fools like you and I'm not doing it any more. You will listen and listen good. DO YOU UNDERSTAND ME!"

It came to me the one thing witches couldn't do was convey to men that's what they were. It was exhausting.

These two successful men, used to authority and power, sat twisting their fingers together like Huey and Dewey confronted by Donald Duck. I lowered my voice.

"Robin will bear me out that I suffered the same bullshit from him for the best part of thirty years. Believe it or not – it was a photograph he'd taken that began to convince him, followed by several illustrations from his daughter and an enforced meeting with his harridan of a mother. That's partly – but not entirely – the reason he looks so wiped-out."

Rob refilled their glasses and looked sympathetic.

I told them first about Jill because her tale was the most straightforward and we'd covered it in previous conversations in any case. I followed this by explaining to Nik he'd been sharing a house with two witches for the past sixteen years and finished with Lena's murders.

If anything, they looked worse than Rob had after his brief trip to the Veil at Dana Point.

Danny began to snigger nervously. I threw a cushion at him and he stopped laughing.

Rob, who had maintained his cool, continued:

"Sorry guys, but she's on the level. Worse is yet to come."

He gave me a quick sideways grin.

His Dad had said the very same to him when my own abilities were first explained by my mother and his.

He coughed, took a swig of his drink and straightened his face.

"We have a way to prove all this to you if you think you can take it."

"Can we go into the garden? I need some air," said Nik - as if that was going to help.

"Sure," said Rob, relieved for once he was in the know and not floundering like his two friends.

How to tackle explaining the situation with Anna, Katy and Greta? If the other side of the Veil was involved I had no chance at all.

"Anna is a Coven witch. On her eighteenth birthday – the 21st of this month – she becomes fully-fledged Wicca."

Nik and Dan looked at each other, completely baffled.

"That means we all – herself included - will learn the full extent of her powers. So far we know she has a limited ability to raise the dead, and my great-grandmother tells me, although it seems to be a bit of a remote possibility to me, she is an Empath. That means she can find the good in people and use it to help them."

"She's also a Kineticist," explained Rob. "That means she can move things around without touching them. Herself included since I've seen her leap walls."

Another top-up of glasses.

"I'll tell you a little about your wife, Nik, to put your mind at rest. She is precisely like me. She can hear and see close friends and relatives who have crossed beyond the Veil – died, that is - but as they are connected to a location, you wouldn't have known. Hers are in Egypt and mine in England – except for my goddam great-grandmother who pops up all over the place."

Witch Ethereal

"Great grandmother?" asked Nik, feebly.

"Yes, her name's <u>Molly</u> Carrick Graham and she died in 1937," said Robbie, his attempt at being helpful falling short.

"And Katy?" asked Nik.

I could see he'd rather not have the answer, but Rob came up with the perfect response when he said:

"Your lass is of the same Egyptian line and can see sparkles and hide herself. Mine raises the dead and jumps on walls like a fairy. Swap you."

"As for the Coven," I said, lying through my teeth, "It only means Anna wants Katy in her group of best friends."

Robin looked at me as if I'd lost my senses so I dug him in the ribs.

He hid his grin behind his glass. It was the first – the very first time - I'd seen him find his situation funny.

Danny, quite rightly, looked as if his whole world had fallen apart. Nobody was who he thought they were, and his intended – he hoped, because she'd sent back the ring – was a dead girl walking.

I knew she couldn't keep her nose out.

Up popped <u>Molly</u> who told me Jill would be his third wife and he'd met his soul-mate. The first of the other two had been a gold-digger. He'd married her when the band was at the peak of their success when he was young and stupid, and the second had a new gigolo in their bed every time he was away from home. <u>Deidra</u>

had cheered him up no end when he was going through the divorce.

I was glad because I knew Jill to be thoughtful, considerate and kind, and much more my idea of an empath than Anna.

I heaved a sigh of relief on two counts. The first that Danny was going to fight for Jill, and the second that Molly had at last visited without offering an incoherent bit of information. I should have known better.

"Anna says Puddy won't be around much longer. Find her her favorite spot in the garden."

She disappeared.

"Molly?" asked Rob, supposing it might as easily be our daughter.

"Just my ancestor speaking up on your behalf, Dan. You and Jill are good."

Chapter Forty-three

Dan and Nik Prepare for a Journey

"Anna had intended you to be at her gig," said Robbie. "I got the impression she wanted as many people as possible there."

He paused to think.

"Odd when you considers she's kept all this under wraps her entire life. Too bad you won't get flights so close to the date. She'll be disappointed."

Nik looked at Dan and Dan looked back. They both grinned.

"On it," said Danny and ran for his car.

Seemed we weren't the only ones with secrets.

We'd stopped hearing from Anna and Katy. Cam and Greta seemed to have disappeared off the face of the earth too, so it was a relief when Cam called us from Bythwaite, although her conversation did nothing to reassure Rob.

He really didn't care if his daughter was the devil or Queen of England as long as she remained his baby. He wanted reassurance and it wasn't forthcoming. Apparently, the girls were all at Smyltandale and Cam was to join them that afternoon. She'd call us then.

Our flight was at 3 a.m.. We waited as long as we were able but didn't hear from her again.

We met Jill in the travelers' lounge at Los Angeles airport. She was about as cross as I'd ever seen her. Apparently Danny who'd been talking to her in words of one syllable since our fateful meeting, had shut her in the bedroom and decided it would be a convenient time to fix their relationship… She couldn't go on, but I rather got the idea. So did Rob. He gave a great guffaw which put paid to every conversation in the lounge. Jill looked miffed and refused to look at him.

To make things worse, Dan had then disappeared completely without a word. He hadn't gone anywhere for long, as the only things she could find missing – she thought – were one leather hold-all, some shirts, a pair of jeans and his toothbrush.

Intriguing but not enough the put her off leaving herself.

Once we'd boarded I said to her.

"Let Rob sit on the aisle side."

"Why?"

"You'll find out."

We didn't hear from Danny and Nik until late evening on the 19th , when they turned up at Scarsdale looking relaxed, dapper and smug.

Witch Ethereal

Dan's band had a private jet which had been in a hanger at Los Angeles airport. Getting it fired up and in the air was no problem when you paid the pilot's wages.

There were hugs and kisses all round. Dan had crossed the Atlantic a few times with Rick Adams to compose and enjoy the seclusion of Smyltandale.

I rather gathered that was where he'd have preferred to go this time, but when Dad took his bag upstairs to a room at Scarsdale, he explained the girls – that was Anna, Katy and Greta – had locked themselves in to the cottage and hadn't been seen again. Cam had stayed chatting to Zella for twenty-four hours then she and Jill had gone to find out what was going on.

They never came back.

If Zella knew what was happening, she wasn't telling. Joe was livid. His daughter had become a hermit and his wife point-blank refused to say why.

As I was brushing out my hair in front of the dressing table mirror that night, and Robbie lay in bed engrossed in my Dad's copy of Farmers' Weekly, I got to thinking.

Anna had succeeded in getting all her loved ones in place as she wanted. I'd never thought it was going to happen but here we all were:

Her beloved Dad and I, Danny and Jill, Nik and Cam, Katy and Greta. She'd also got her Grandma and <u>Grandad Greenwood</u> and Uncle Joe whether she liked it or not. I was hopeful characters from beyond the Veil would be there as well: <u>Molly</u> – who never missed a thing – <u>Claire,</u> and I hoped desperately for Robbie's sake, <u>Deidra</u>. I was less certain of <u>Grandads Robert and Josh</u> and <u>Dermot</u>. Perhaps it was an event important enough for gender to be waived. If it was, Joe, Dad, Nik and Danny were in for a shock.

But it wasn't the only shock which occurred on August 19th.

Chapter Forty-four
Malignant Forces

Molly whispered in my ear in the early morning light and we walked in the yard as she gave me my instructions.

We were to go to Bythwaite and assemble at the Sisters no later than midnight that night – the twentieth. I'd to arrange all those that side, she'd do the rest.

What rest? Molly double-speak again.

By three in the afternoon it was clear we weren't going to see our daughters – or Nik and Dan's better halves – so I took time out to walk the hay meadow path to see if I could find Grandad Josh at the bottom of the wheatfield near the river.

I didn't hold out much hope because of my years of absence but at least I'd get some solitude and fresh air.

He was there – blue and cheerful as ever – with his habitual welcoming grin.

"Chuffin' exciting night to come. Tha's no idea."

He jumped up and down with glee.

"Not a clue if my lasses'll let us see, but it's always what I've wanted for thee. You, Mol Carrick, your mam, Mrs. O'Connor, Mrs. Claire – you all deserve it."

"What about Anna – it's her birthday after all - and the Girls?" I asked, laughing.

"Aye, indeed. What about them Girls? What indeed!"

And with that, he was gone.

I'd just turned to walk back to the house, wondering exactly which girls he'd meant, when my attention was caught by a slight movement amongst the trees on the river bank.

Thinking one of our daughters had taken time out for fresh air, I walked over to take a look. Perhaps it was Cam…or Jill? Either way it would be good to see them.

I set off at a trot and moved the foliage away on the bank. Before I could pull away, a hand shot out from between the bushes and grabbed my wrist. There was quiet, malevolent laughter and a low voice said:

"I couldn't have planned it better! I'd hoped to get the brat but you'll do just as well – better maybe. Your family took one of mine, I'll take one of you," said Lena belligerently. "Eye for an eye, tooth for a tooth.

She laughed again but this time it was lighter, more amused.

Lena – Lena *Michaels*. She was getting as bad as my great gran for turning up unexpected and unwanted.

"I wonder what turn fate will take this time?" she mused, referring to the hand I'd shaken loose from my wrist. We've had a broken neck and a drowning. If your damn daughter hadn't been there," she spat, "they'd both be across the Veil and out of the way.

"Perhaps, since we're here, it'll be the river. Your family has a penchant for death by water as I recall. Lady Anna locked away on her own business? What a shame. Great birthday present for her to find her mother, one part lodged under the bridge outside her cottage, and the other long gone beyond the Veil."

Her laughter this time was bitter.

"Poor recompense for taking my daughter."

"What the hell are you talking about. I've no idea who your daughter is."

"Oh, you do. Search your heart and you'll find the answer."

Oh God, <u>Josh Greenwood</u> Mark 2.

There was that slight pop and <u>Molly</u> was hovering over the rushing water behind Lena and sneering with distain.

I looked to her for help, but she turned away and disappeared.

"Your husband killed my daughter. Think about it, and in the meantime I suggest you walk away from the river."

She pointed to the house, then waded to the other side of the torrent and disappeared amongst the undergrowth. No way was I going to follow her. I'd been ill-wished.

I'd no idea if it was my Wicca strain which went back generations, or protection from beyond the Veil, but all that happened on the way back was that I again twisted the wrist weakened on the ocean shore when I was looking for Rob, As if to emphasize Lena's hex, I caught my foot in a rabbit hole and knackered my ankle again.

Still expecting another disaster, I spoke to Rob in the privacy of our room and explained what had happened.

"Give it to me word for word," he said, scratching his brow.

"It could be Layla I suppose – she's the only one not close to us I can think of who's died, and I was there soon after she fell. But I didn't push her over the waterfall, and she couldn't possibly be Lena's daughter. She'd be too old."

"Not likely," I agreed. "There must be a lesson in this for me somewhere because Molly wouldn't help me."

"Typical."

Why Lena Michaels had travelled all the way from Los Angeles to a remote corner of England was puzzling. She'd been vicious about my family which made me nervous, although she'd be no match for Anna as had already been made apparent. But as had also been seen by Lena, Anna wasn't with me – she was locked away at Smyltandale.

Could it matter that this must have been the largest gathering of witches for decades if not centuries? But then, what could a Wicca of dubious abilities hope to accomplish?

The sun was beginning to sink behind the fells and the shadows to lengthen. We'd to be there in a few hours. At least <u>Molly</u> did bother to tell me that.

"Stick close. Lena might not have finished with you," whispered Rob.

"She didn't do much to you and you were her target. You only knocked over a plant."

"It was a Ming pot worth thousands – Nik told me afterwards."

As we walked down to the living room, his arm round my shoulders, he kissed me lightly on the lips and we both fell downstairs.

Anna's guests were still ensconced at Smyltandale and it was clear they'd be travelling to the Sisters from there.

<u>Molly</u> had left the Bythwaite arrangements to me and Mum, so as it was a much easier walk from there, Mum and Dad, Dan, Nik, Rob and I departed Scarsdale in a cavalcade to meet Zella and Joe. Altogether, two witches of sorts, four sceptics and two innocent enthusiasts, congregated in the hall at Bythwaite.

On the wall, I was distracted by a faded photograph of <u>Molly</u> and the ghastly picture of the pack bridge at Smyltandale I'd painted years before.

From Smyltandale we could expect one potential super-star, one old hand and three novice witches.

Could we expect guests from beyond the Veil? Neither Molly nor Granddad Josh – the only ones of my dead people I'd seen so far on this visit – hadn't said, but then I'd been too preoccupied to ask.

We crossed the stile opposite the farm gate and walked the earthen path to the Sisters. The higher we climbed the stronger the breeze became.

Rob took my hand. Bathed in moonlight, my husband was Heathcliffe again, wild and romantic.

Chapter Forty-five
The Gathering

I don't know what I'd been expecting but it certainly wasn't a bare hillside with seven plus one standing stones, tall and inscrutable, lit by Selene's orb – the moon to the uninitiated.

Nothing moved – even the biting wind had stopped and the reeds stood motionless. There were no haunting bird cries, even our footsteps were muted.

"So what now?" said Dan – then winced as his voice, volume enhanced by the unnatural silence, echoed down the slope and across the quiet hills.

"Perhaps you could record your next album up here," suggested Rob.

"No electricity," Dan considered, deep in thought.

"They'll be expecting us to know what's going on," I whispered in Mum's ear, "Any ideas?"

She shrugged.

"Not a clue. All we can do is wait – something'll happen soon enough, even if it's just the curlews calling to make it feel a bit less like a graveyard."

"Not a clever thing to say when we can probably expect a contingent of the dead."

"Oops! sorry…"

As if to echo our conversation, Nik said:

"Where're my wife and daughter? If I don't see them in the next half hour I'll be looking for them myself. Your daughter won't be feeling so good when I've finished. She started all this."

I looked heavenward.

For his own well-being – and everyone else's no doubt - that would be the worst possible thing he could do. He could end up with fingers growing out of his ears.

"Just give it a bit longer – Molly, said midnight. It's only ten-to."

"No!" thundered Dan. "Molly again? You keep talking about her as if she was someone I should know."

As if by magic – pardon me – up she popped.

"Stand them over there out of the way, across from the big Sister, Meg. Keep them away from the path. And tell them if they value their lives to keep quiet. Pray hard none of them are scared of fireworks."

"Can't you just let them see the Veil people, Molly? It would make my life so much easier." I groaned.

"Oh, alright," she said reluctantly, "seeing as how I'm going to show myself to Anastasia anyway."

"Anastasia?"

"Tonight is a night of formality – and maiden names. Meg becomes Margaret Graham, you are Angela Greenwood, Cam becomes Sharina Cameron. And there's some woman called Talibah Cameron. Don't ask – don't know, other than that she's of the blood.

Witch Ethereal

"She's Cam's sister. Married a bloke from Colorado. She and Cam are half-Egyptian – their father's from Kilmarnock."

"Egyptian? Strong vibes…good," said Molly with her usual lack of clarity. "And a Scot too – even better."

Molly Carrick had been a Scot herself, of course. Fortunately, she stopped short of dancing a highland fling at the mention of a fellow countryman, although I saw it did cross her mind.

"Not the time or place," she said, straightening her skirt and her face. "Now, where was I? Oh yes…

"The rest of them have no problems," she carried on regardless, "with surnames anyway, but Christian names should be observed so – she looked at a barely decipherable slip of transparent paper – there's Robin, Nicholas and Daniel……Not that anyone'll bother talking to them."

"Get a crack on, Mol……sorry, Mary. It's knocking midnight," said a familiar voice.

When Robbie came to, his head on my knee, his spectral mother looked down at him with distain.

He grinned at her and she tutted and stalked off, calling back over her shoulder.

"Tha'll be the deeth o' me…"

Deidra had never been fair with her youngest son. For love of us both, he had proved his metal over and over – far beyond what could reasonably have been expected. Added to which, his daughter was about to become……

Here I'd to stop since it occurred to me I had no clue what she was about to become. No doubt I was about to find out.

A degree of sanity was restored when Claire arrived, except that I burst into tears. I'd forgotten what a beauty she was and how graceful. Everyone who had ever known her loved her, apart from her bastard of a husband, and she'd fixed him herself with a shotgun.

My mother appeared at her shoulder beaming from ear to ear. The two of them, and Rob's mother Deidra had always been the closest of companions.

To see the three of them together again, albeit in two dimensions did my heart good – Rob's too. All those he loved had come together on a bleak hillside in Westmoreland: his mother, his Aunt Claire and me, the wife he'd chased half way across the world to win. My mother, who'd always treated him with amused affection was in there somewhere too, I had no doubt. All that was missing was Anna.

There was a short buzz like a swarm of angry bees. One by one around the stone circle a dozen flaming torches burst into life.

A small table rose from the exact center of the circle. The whole thing was composed of vertical crystals of shimmering amethyst, but the top was polished to such a shine it reflected the image of a large box. I was too far away to be sure but it looked like ivory, intricately carved.

Witch Ethereal

Beside <u>Molly</u> at the table stood my mother, oddly transparent – in fact, exactly like <u>Claire</u> whose hand she held – and <u>Deidra</u>.

Shocked, I searched out my Dad amongst the little group of onlookers. He looked surprised but not concerned. He'd no experience of my dead people and had denied their existence my whole life.

He and Uncle Joe were going to have to reconsider – it would be devastatingly difficult for them. Yet before our eyes stood mother, wife and sister – <u>Margaret Graham Greenwood</u> - smiling at us benignly with her finger to her lips for silence.

She looked so happy. Around the splendid table were ranged three women who shared a soul – and the ubiquitous <u>Molly</u>, their mentor.

The air was suddenly bone-shatteringly cold, and the torches flared bright enough to be seen from both Bythwaite and Scarsdale. From icy, the air became searingly hot, before the torches settled into steady flame and it became pleasantly warm.

It was like a fanfare without sound.

A gentle whirring gradually increased in pace and volume, then abruptly, it ceased.

From each stone in turn, beginning with the largest, a figure began to emerge, appearing at first to be composed of the moss and ancient crustacea of the rock.

Gradually increasing in clarity, before each monolith, emerged women whose height matched those of the stones behind them. They ranged in size from the pugnacious figure of Maggie McGowan right down to little Jeannie Thompson, scar and all.

These were the very same women <u>Molly</u> had introduced me to in the cave at Dana Point, where Anna had rescued her father with their help.

They stood solemnly facing, still as statues, the figures gathered around the amethyst table.

An array of gob-smacked men – and me who wasn't, but still as much in the dark as they, stood in a group, waiting.

There was a significant pause, then more figures began to appear, this time from the direction of the scree slope above Scarsdale.

First Anna, and behind her, Cam and her sister – her absolute double, Katy and Greta. I was amazed to see Jill amongst them. She had no trace of the blood, so far as I knew.

All stark naked.

I heard pronounced gasps from Nik, Dan, Joe and my Dad,

The young women were quite beautiful, with skin like alabaster lit warmly from within. Cam and Tally shone softly gold in the torchlight.

Chapter Forty-six

An Awakening a Long Time Coming

As they neared the table, Anna strode forward, her hair a mane of soft tresses a-glitter with shining points of golden light and falling below her waist.

She looked imperious, but I was glad to see there was kindness and love in her eyes as she bowed gracefully to her grandmother, and with a small shock of recognition to <u>Molly</u> who'd been bending her ear her entire life, but who she'd never seen. It made her smile and <u>Molly</u> winked at her.

<u>Deidra</u> and <u>Claire</u> she hadn't known, so her greeting was more formal.

I glanced at the men and saw they'd been joined by my granddads. Josh grinned and waved as usual, finding it difficult to contain his glee.

Of the rest, Dan and Nik were gawping, stunned, particularly at partners they'd never to that moment known. Joe and my Dad could only be described as staggered. By what was difficult to gauge, since almost all of the proceedings before them they'd poopooed as impossible for a lifetime.

I came close to cheering – vindicated at last!

My mother and father gazed at each other. I saw tears begin to slide down his face as the reality of her passing dawned. Theirs had been a true love-match and now they would be apart for the very first time. I saw my mother mouth to him 'soon', her face wreathed in smiles. He nodded bravely, knowing full well, when all this was over, he'd have a funeral to arrange.

As I was paying attention to all the people who had had a part in my happy life, it suddenly came to me that everyone seemed to have a purpose there, but for Rob and me who were standing twiddling our thumbs.

Not to be conceited or anything, but we had given life to this mystical paragon. I'd have thought we'd have been offered a chair at least.

A seat there was, if not the one I'd envisaged and not for me.

It wasn't much of a chair. Looking rather like something from a Sunday School but carved in one piece of light wood, it appeared and settled, seemingly of its own volition, between Anna and the box on the table.

As she sat, it wobbled slightly under her weight.

I could see the shock in her eyes, concealed from all but those who knew her best. This wasn't what she'd been expecting either.

All this surprise was only helping to exacerbate the giggling Rob was trying to contain. He'd slunk behind me out of the way but I could feel him shaking with laughter at the bursting of a fair number of bubbles belonging to the Graham and Greenwood families.

"You might well laugh," I whispered over my shoulder, "Until a few weeks ago you'd have been turned into a pillar of salt as well."

Witch Ethereal

The same deathly hush descended on the enclosure again. All conversation ceased. Even the crackle of the torches, to that point clearly audible, stopped.

Molly began a long, tedious and pompous diatribe peppered with words like 'magical power', 'responsibility' and 'never before' until all the wonder of the moment had melted like the spirits themselves and even Grandad Greenwood was nodding. The Sisters stood still as statues. Perhaps they'd been part of the stones so long they'd forgotten how to bend in the middle.

"Rob!" I exclaimed, dumfounded, "Look! She's solid!"

It seemed an inadequate way to point out, whether or not she was spirit, Molly was now as densely present as the on-lookers. This was a magic I knew nothing of.

It occurred to me the Sisters may have had some hand in this, since their eyes, until that moment as tightly closed as they'd been on the morning of Rob's death, flashed open and all, bright as lasers, were firmly fixed on Molly.

She opened the box on the amethyst table and took out a small silver charger set with colored stones – precious no doubt. Tipping into it the contents of a pouch, Molly walked to the closest torch and set fire to it.

"God!" exclaimed Rob, stepping forwards in astonishment, "She'd giving her marijuana……she'd drugging her!"

Witch Ethereal

Molly had indeed walked over to Anna and was wafting the smoke from the dish under her nose. I saw her eyes flutter and close but she remained upright, stiffening against the chair back.

Jill, Cam and Tally retained their composure, but I saw the young girls look at each other in consternation.

I took a fleeting moment to glance around the circle to see what was happening amongst the on-lookers. With the exception of the Wicca, this side of the Veil or beyond, they appeared all to be gazing straight ahead, with their eyes closed, swapping places with the Sisters. Clearly, the rest of the ceremony wasn't for them. I was surprised, therefore, that both Jill and Rob were wide awake. How could that be?

When I looked back again, Rob was thunderstruck, and I saw Anna had opened her eyes, turned her head and was looking, unblinking, straight at us.

This was no longer my Anna. The graveyard look in her eyes which had so hypnotized Rob and me when she'd flung us against the stones to shut us up, had intensified. This was no mere Coven witch – this was a woman, terrifying in her power.

With no effort from me, I began to walk forward towards her and couldn't look away. Robin appeared to be doing the same but I couldn't turn my head to see. My eyes were fixed on hers.

This should have felt like hypnotism except that I was wide awake and keenly aware of what was happening.

Witch Ethereal

No – not hypnotism – this was magic. She was bringing us to her. When we reached her she released us and took us both by the hand, kissing Rob then me on the palm.

Her long tresses were now covered with stars, which shone as brightly as the Milky Way Rob had so loved to watch on Huntington Beach when he was feeling at his lowest.

Molly said:

"It is given to the Lady to choose who sets the crown on her head. She has chosen *you,* which if I might say so, shows a deal of common sense."

Deidra coughed, then laughed at the disrespectful remark.

"For once in thy life, tha's done the right thing, Robin O'Connor! Not only rich as Croesus, but now you've fathered Queen Mab here. You've done me proud......beggin' your pardon, granddaughter...or is it yer Majesty?"

Mum trod on her foot to shut her up as in days gone by.

If Anna had cast a spell over us, it disappeared in a flash as she fought hard to maintain her dignity. She would have loved Deidra. Perhaps at some distant point she might still.

"No," said Molly, reading my mind, "She's immortal until she decides to hand back the crown. It only took me five generations before I got sick and tired of it all.

Witch Ethereal

You can't imagine how delighted I was when you brought Anastasia here to see me."

What!

"You'd been Queen! Oh, my God, <u>Molly</u>, I've cursed you up hill and down dale my entire life."

"Think nothing of it…"

Of course, we'd been talking across 'Queen Mab', which wouldn't have sat right with her in Torrance, never mind at her Coronation.

"Enough!" she commanded, and her stars twinkled brighter. "We've a job to do here and afterwards I've some business of my own to conclude. First, give these girls some clothes before they freeze to death."

A pile of gold-fringed cloaks of velvet and in a variety of colors, appeared as if by magic and her attendants weren't slow in wrapping themselves.

Instead of velvet, Anna's own cloak was composed of a net of tiny stars – a coat of many colors. Twinkling from its threads shone spangles of red and gold, pink, purple and silver. When she pulled her long hair from the collar she was resplendent from head to foot. A glittering shower of light.

"Can we do something about this goddamn chair <u>Molly</u>? It's bruising my posterior."

Somethings never change. Rob, not one for being overawed, chuckled.

The chair instantly disappeared and in its place stood a throne of transparent crystal, which shocked the socks off him.

"Come on, come on...let's get on with this, they're not all immortal," said Anna, indicating the rigid statues which until recently had been on-lookers.

"Daddy...you stand there...and Momma this side."

My hand buzzed as she took it and I heard the distant song of the Seven Sisters, who, expressions now benign stood smiling down at us, until Anna flicked her wrist and consigned them to their individual monoliths. As their fixed stares disappeared, Molly returned to her spectral form. Seemed settling their blessings on the new Queen had been their purpose – and it had been worth seeing.

Molly coughed, cracked her fingers and unlocked the ivory box on the indigo surface of the table.

When she lifted the lid, a flash of lightening shot out, striking sparks from the table and throwing the faces grouped around the circle into sharp relief. Everyone except Anna and Molly, who was scrabbling about in the bottom of the box, took several steps backwards, but craned their necks to see what was within.

Chapter Forty-seven
Trial and Retribution

This was the crowning of a Queen and a Queen of Magic at that. What would the crown be like? Would it be composed of stars like Anna's cloak, or jewels like that of the English Queen.

In actual fact, it turned out to be a wreath of green leaves, tied with a satin ribbon.

"Myrtle and bay," said Molly, "gifted by the Man of Green, the King of Nature himself. Myrtle is for Devotion and Love, and Bay holds the secrets of Wisdom and Healing. With these at your command who needs mere rubies and sapphires?"

She handed the coronet to me and my fingers tingled from the magic it contained. I passed it straight to Rob, who she loved above all else, and he looked at us both in turn. For the first time in his life he could think of not one thing to say or do.

"Oh, for the love of God, get on with it," said his mother, "Time's a-wasting."

If she'd had a watch she'd have been tapping it.

Robin kissed his daughter on the brow and rubbed his cheek against hers, before placing the wreath on curls so similar to his own. I watched as each leaf transformed into purest gold.

Witch Ethereal

Anastasia O'Connor, tall and regal stood before us, mistress of all she surveyed.

"She's all-powerful," whispered <u>Molly</u> although the truth of that was apparent to those with eyes to see.

"Right," said the all-powerful Anna O'Connor, "Back to business."

She sat on the throne and arranged her stars around her in a purposeful manner.

I'd always been aware she was an organized person but I'd never for one moment dreamed she could sit naked through a Coronation then hold an Assize. That was impressive.

"There're only two items on the agenda, mother. Don't fret."

We were all going to have to be so careful with our thoughts from now on.

"First item – my Coven.

"The usual thing for a Queen has always been to put together her Coven before the Coronation. I'm aiming for quality rather than quantity since I intend drawing on my witches powers frequently. So, I am prepared to convey powers on Jill Perkins who will become keeper of Retribution.

"I confer this blessing on her because her character can handle it……and also, because I intend drawing on it a fair bit in years to come. How she explains it to her

Witch Ethereal

husband-to-be may take a bit of ingenuity and I wish her the best of luck."

She beckoned Jill forward, placed a hand on her forehead and we mortals toppled over from a shaking of the earth which must have registered six on the Richter Scale.

Jill, who didn't appear to have felt a thing, dropped to her knees, and looking at Anna with adoration, took her proffered hand and kissed it, laying it for a moment to her cheek before rising and backing away, for all the world like a medieval courtier.

"Now," intoned Anna regally – well, almost – "Daddy, come over here."

Rob walked over at his normal speed but did none of the kneeling business. This was his daughter – how could he kneel at the feet of his own daughter – it'd look silly.

"Shut it, Deidra," said Anna extending a regal finger, "He stopped being your son when you passed the Veil. He's my Dad now, and *I* call the shots."

Rob laughed out loud. He'd been waiting for someone to say that his entire life.

"Daddy, I've loved you all my life but even I can't make you a woman – and that's the only way you can be a witch. So, I'll up the ante with Momma. She'll be able to call on me and whatever I'm doing, I'll stop and look after you both."

The affection emanating from her increased the intensity of her sparkles and for a moment she was bathed in light.

"Love does that to you," whispered Molly in my ear.

"Sherina, Talibah, Catherine, Jill and Margaret-Claire, you will be the beginnings of my Coven and I will call on your abilities as required, although I won't need your help to see the dead unfortunately." She stared at Molly, who stared back.

No dissent from the ladies, who also did the backwards walk.

"Now to the other matter."

The fell rumbled again, and I heard a torrent of scree rattling down the hillside behind me.

A figure emerged between the stones.

The torch light was so bright, at first I didn't recognize who it was, but as she walked forward and the wind whipped her skirt about her legs, and tugged at her hair I recognized the figure from the cliff top the night my Robbie had died.

Robin heard my whimper and ran back to my side. We faced her together. Cam, who'd believed Lena to be her friend, looked on distraught.

Anna, of course, had known at the time who she was – I remembered the pewter glimmer of her hair.

"Here. Stand right here," she ordered a terrified Lena, who had lost command of her legs as we had earlier.

"Explain yourself."

There was a prolonged and very awkward pause.

"Well...get on with it!" prodded Anna.

"That sonofabitch killed my daughter!"

She leered at Robbie.

"How? Which daughter?"

"You know – my Layla. You know he shoved her over a waterfall and she died. She loved him and he deserted her – turned her to drink and drugs. Even so she never would have killed herself. Not my Layla."

Were they talking about the same person?

"Wasn't she a bit old to be your daughter? If she was, you must have just been in your teens when she was born."

Anna, of course, knew all the answers to this but was indulging the rest of us – especially her Dad – in a bit of theatre.

Lena looked less confident.

"I was twelve. The baby was taken from me at the hospital. I only found Layla just before she died.

"I found her when you did. Same day, same place," she said to me, sobbing now. "Later I was there when she fell over the waterfall. I hid in the trees. He pushed her."

This last she spat at Rob, anger overcoming grief.

"And are you sure of this? You must have been yards away when it happened."

"I'm certain. He thought he was onto a good thing before he was found out. Then he'd to be rid of her.

"It was before she and that guy who works for him…" me and Al "…arrived. There was no-one else around

Witch Ethereal

for miles. The three of you must have worked out a plan to hush it up later. He's rich – it'd be easy."

I winced. You didn't accuse the father of the Queen of Witches of being complicit in a murder, no matter how upset you were.

Rob was looking indignant but Anna waved her hand and he was mute.

"Molly, come here," ordered Anna. "Confess."

Molly stood before the throne looking at her feet, no doubt thinking of a way she could wriggle out of this. It was long since she'd felt contrite about anything.

"There's no way out," said Anna.

She leaned back and said:

"I know you thought you were acting in our best interests but there's a lesson to be learned. My mother explained it was wrong to send people across the Veil, even when they've committed the worst of crimes. They've to learn from what they've done."

I saw Granddad Greenwood nodding sagely in agreement.

"Eye for an eye, tooth for a tooth," sneered Lena.

"Poof! That attitude went out with the Israelites. Grow up!"

Then, turning her head slowly and with great dignity, the Lady continue:

"Well, Molly?"

Witch Ethereal

"I did it. She was messing with my family. She'd split up my great granddaughter and her husband and was trying to take away their daughter – you!"

"Nonetheless you should have let it play out. There was nothing she could do to me and it might have avoided the damage to my father."

One or two of the onlookers exchanged surprised glances.

Their Lady grasped the arms of the throne and stood, magnificent in her fury.

"She pushed Robin O'Connor – who gave me life – over a cliff and he died. Molly is exonerated for understanding the situation and aiding me in resurrecting him."

There is no justice on earth to match magical retribution. The judge in this case already knew the answers before the questions were asked.

Despite the seriousness of the situation, I came close to laughing out loud at the expression on Deidra's face. Anna's lips twitched as she read my mind.

This bastard woman had put her in the position of booting her son back into the land of the living, which was the last thing she wanted to do.

She pushed up her gossamer sleeves and the look on her face alone would have knocked Lena dead had she been on this side of the Veil.

"Mrs. O'Connor can't correct the damage you did to her son, so just this once, we'll adopt your attitude to justice.

Witch Ethereal

"By the laws of Nature and the Wicca World you are condemned to consider your actions under their jurisdiction until you understand the enormity of your many misdemeanors – oh and the paltry powers you possess will be removed from this moment on."

Anna closed her eyes. Her magical light intensified and her lips moved.

Any other witch would have been chanting a spell, but I knew with Anna this was much more.

She was communing with the power of nature itself.

The turf around Lena's feet became the same iridescent green circle she'd scratched from the earth as a baby at Santa Barbara.

She cast me a sidelong glance and smiled at our shared memory.

Slowly, at first almost imperceptibly, tendrils poked through the ground at the perimeter of the small emerald circle, twisting and thickening ever upwards until Lena was imprisoned in tree roots which met a foot above her head and intertwined.

Then the earth shuddered as the cage with its captive, was sucked beneath the ground and the bright circle she'd been standing on faded again to its natural color.

"My Queen……" exclaimed a shocked voice from the group of onlookers.

Anna flicked her cape behind her,

"I'm Head Witch and don't you ever forget it. Queens live in palaces – I live in every star, blade of grass, every bird, flower and breeze. I see everything, hear everything, feel everything and retribution is swift. Now I'm going home – I suggest you do the same."

She nodded at Rob, who had been released, and me.

Before us all, she shone blindingly for a moment before blending with the dawn.

As she melded into the light of the rising sun, those excluded from the night's happenings were released from their stupor.

The only thing remaining was the crystal throne and on its seat were four gold rings inscribed with names:

Daniel Charlton, Nicholas Chilton, Guy Greenwood, Joseph Graham.

And a note on a bit of paper torn from a note-book which read:

"Wear them and give us no more grief."

Epilogue

Part One

The rings had two immediate effects.

The wearers appeared to have dropped dead. There was no sign of breathing and they went cold and waxen.

Danny was the first to go, which was probably as well as he was the least connected to our world, or at least had been until an hour earlier, and also the most belligerent. So when he lay like a reject from Madame Tussaud's, there were not a few breaths of relief.

"Like hell I'm doing that!" pronounced Nik until the ring was forced onto his finger by his wife. Cam couldn't wipe the grin off her face, even when gentle Katy appeared at her side and begged her to be more sympathetic.

Joe and Dad went quietly. It had become such a habit to deny any supernatural happenings in their lives they no doubt assumed Anna had left them some pretty trinkets.

They grinned at each other, put on the rings and fell to the ground, poleaxed like the others.

Anna, empathy missing as usual, had knocked them out with none of the kindness she'd shown her father. No doubt they were being educated in dreams by their own friends and relatives across the Veil, and would return with fleas in their ears, as Robbie had.

"A couple of hours to spare," said my husband from experience, as he looked down on their ashen faces. He checked his watch.

"Let's go eat – the spooks can clean up, and the guys can totter down on their own as and when."

"Your lack of concern is shameful given the treatment you demanded when it was your turn."

"Yeah, sure…sorry," Rob said grinning.

Over coffee we watched them return, trundling down the hill in the twilight: Nik confused, Joe furious and Dan, turning to Jill for comfort, the biggest sap for all his bravado.

On our return to Scarsdale, I found my poor father leaning over the gate feeding sweet grass to a couple of lambs.

I'd expected him to be overcome with grief, but although pale and serious, he was in complete command of himself.

He'd driven home with my mother's body, that of his beloved wife, and laid her gently on their bed. He'd found her on the very same spot at the top of the ridge overlooking Scarsdale where he'd first kissed her years before.

I'd attended funerals before – <u>Claire's, Deidra's and Dermot's</u> – but never was there a sweeter affair than

Witch Ethereal

that of my darling mother. Not many witches had the presence of their Lady at their passing. Even if she drew on Katy's skill of invisibility, I knew she was there. I felt her hand on my shoulder and her kiss on my cheek. I knew Rob did too. His grief was for the loss of his daughter, not his mother-in-law.

The burial of Meg Graham Greenwood was attended by both the living and the dead. On one side of the Veil her loss was mourned, on the other celebrated.

While it was true she was a witch of meagre powers, Margaret Graham Greenwood could, for her goodness, call to her the beautiful things of the air - red admirals, painted lady butterflies, kingfishers, larks and the melodious blackbird.

The only other minor witch I'd ever known – Lena – had, by contrast, used her powers to inflict harm and instill fear, and had been imprisoned beneath the earth until such time as she'd learned her lesson.

Rob and I visited the Sisters one last time before we left. Neither of us said anything but we both knew there was only one more trip to be made – for my Dad. Other than that, our days on English soil were done.

When it was Joe and Zella's time we wouldn't be needed. Greta would bear the weight of their passing.

We flew home to Los Angeles, subdued. Our lives had changed completely on that fellside in Westmoreland.

I'd lost my mother to the Veil, and our daughter had, in more ways than one, risen to a realm high above our understanding.

While I understood the gift she'd conferred on me, it wouldn't be appropriate to call on her unless there was great need. I didn't anticipate that would be often.

Rob was no less unwell than usual on a flight, but quiet and discreet about it which was a first.

I could say nothing to sooth his distress. He'd loved his daughter more than his own life.

He'd a habit of confusing personalities, as he had with my adult and childhood selves before we were married. In some way I think Anna had taken over from Deidra in his heart. She was just as domineering in her own way, and Robbie was a gentle soul who would always bring out the caring side of a woman – Lena excepted. But Lena had had the makings of a psychopath, so she didn't count.

Although my heart bled for him, we couldn't live the rest of our lives like this, so after I'd been jolly as long as I could, I closed my eyes, slept and let him be as miserable as he wanted.

When I woke again, he was half way through a double whisky.

Epilogue

Part Two

My Dad's death, when it came the following year, was hardly a surprise. He missed Mum terribly – neither his beloved animals nor the towering fells could distract him. He just seemed to fade away.

Of course, Rob and I were there for the burial, although we arrived two days too late to see him this side of the Veil.

He was laid to rest next to his wife in the churchyard at Nethershaw. The funeral was a quiet affair unlike the bells and whistles accorded to the O'Connors and my mother. He was a painfully shy man, he would have hated the fuss.

Before we left, I visited Dad's grave alone, and tucked mums wedding ring beneath the turf - a better gift from their daughter than a bouquet, no matter how flamboyant. I didn't see any of my people. For me they were across the Veil unseen.

Rob and I climbed Gastal Fell afterwards where we could weep in private – he as well as me. He had a tender heart, and the passing of my parents would stay with him for the rest of his life.

The sadness of a loved-one's passing is all pervasive. Grief and loss flow over and around all things familiar and loved. The cottage at Ghyll Howe would always contain Deidra's spirit, as the fells would take my father's. When Joe's time came I knew he and Dad would walk the fells together as they had in life for as long as it pleased them both.

Anna seemed to have completely disappeared. Neither of us spoke of it – Rob's pain was terrible, and neither of us wanted to speak of her for fear of making the heartache worse.

The shadows beneath the pier at Redondo Beach were still and silent at twilight. I sat alone between the pilings where the salty swell of the ocean met the shore. My parents were gone, my daughter was gone, my husband might as well have gone. We hadn't had a decent conversation since we got home.

Molly did at least have the decency to give us a bit of space to grieve, although as she could flit back and forth across the Veil, death had little significance for her. It was too good to last.

Pop!

"God, you look awful! What on earth's wrong with you?"

Could there ever, in the history of the world, have been such a stupid and insensitive question?

"If you can't say anything useful - bugger off, Molly. I don't have time for your crap just now."

Witch Ethereal

I thought I'd got a handle on my emotions but my chin began to wobble and my eyes to leak.

Pop!

She was gone again. I couldn't say I was sorry.

I went home again with dragging feet and a heavy heart. Rob should have been back from work. He'd need a meal.

At the house door, I paused with my hand on the handle, sighed, and pasted on my happy face.

Usually, if I'd gone out, when I returned he'd either be in his darkroom finishing up some photographs or flicking thoughtlessly through the tv channels.

This time he was doing neither. I began to feel uneasy. His state of mind wasn't exactly stable.

I ran round the house looking for him. Nothing, so I tried the garden.

When I found him I was so relieved – even more so that he was with Anna. He was standing chatting to her at the birdfeeder. She had a pearl-grey rain dove sitting on her finger. Robbie was laughing with her and more animated than I'd seen him for months.

And she…she was just alight with sparkles from head to foot, which, of course he was unaware of. There'd been some serious magic going on.

They both turned to me as I drew closer, both smiling.

"See whose here?"

He hugged me and swung me round

"It's Anna!"

"No shit," I said, through my tears.

I hugged her tightly and kissed her cheek, laughing and crying by turns.

Robbie turned to look at the little bird again and began to stroke its soft feathers. It bent its head in pleasure at his touch.

Anna gave me a meaningful look and whispered in my head:

"Beautiful, isn't it? It's a rain dove."

Then she stared at me with those deep, deep eyes until I felt my knees begin to weaken.

"Did you know its other name is the mourning dove?"

Oh shit! Not Robbie…please God, not my Robbie. Her message was unmistakable.

Of course she knew the words flying round my brain so she continued:

"<u>Molly</u> came. She said you were sitting under the pier next to a dead fish, and of the two of you, the fish looked healthier."

What is it about dead people – why did they only develop a sense of humor when they'd crossed over?

Aloud she said to her Dad:

"All this appearing and disappearing is wearing me out. Go and put the kettle on, please."

Witch Ethereal

At least she said please – otherwise it would have sounded like an order.

When he was out of earshot and the bird had flown away, she took me by the arm and the two of us sat on the garden seat.

"Why are you all sparkly?"

"As I already told you, Molly came – not only her voice – all of her. When she saw you crying on the beach, it occurred to her something was badly wrong. It wasn't that you were sitting on wet sand, or even that you were crying. She had a presentiment something was about to happen. Well, it did.

Thank God – not me and not Rob. Joe? Zella, one of the Coven?

The sparkles were very gradually beginning to dim so I knew the event had passed.

"He did it again."

"Who did? Did what? Damn Anna, is being obtuse a prerequisite of being Head Witch? You're turning into Molly."

She gave me an imperious look.

"Dad. He died again. But I got to him this time so we didn't have all the palaver of ocean caves and the Seven Sisters. I promised I'd come if you needed me and I did. Theia warned me, so I got here in plenty of time.

"He was laying on the grass under the birdfeeder, dead as a dodo when I arrived. Heart attack. Looks pretty good now compared to half an hour ago."

What do you say to that? How do you come to terms with the fact your husband died, yet was standing in the garden stroking a bird?

I ran to the house, dragged Robin into my arms and kissed him over and over until he pushed me away in alarm – so I punched him instead.

"What's your problem? Somebody died?"

Anna had strolled after me and stood watching us with that 'parents are so dim' look on her face

"He doesn't know?" I asked silently.

"Nope – no idea. I'm an Empath. I knew he'd probably have another heart attack if I told him. I suggest you hold off for a while too."

Robbie, oblivious to our mute conversation, put an arm round both of us. He kissed each of us on the forehead but before he could speak Anna whispered:

"I had to bring him back. You share a soul. Neither of you could live without the other and I'm not ready to be an orphan.

"I have to warn you though. I'm in trouble with the Green Man. He thought bringing Dad back once was pushing it. He's going to be furious now – even I can't mess with nature – well, not much. There won't be a third time so wrap him in cotton-wool."

"Bubble-wrap," I said, accidentally aloud.

Witch Ethereal

Anna's expression softened.

"One thing I will promise you faithfully. The next time, you won't be separated. You'll cross the Veil together – but Theia tells me that's a bit away yet.

"Where's that cuppa, Dad," prodded Anastasia Deidra O'Conner, Queen and Witch Supreme, "I'm parched."

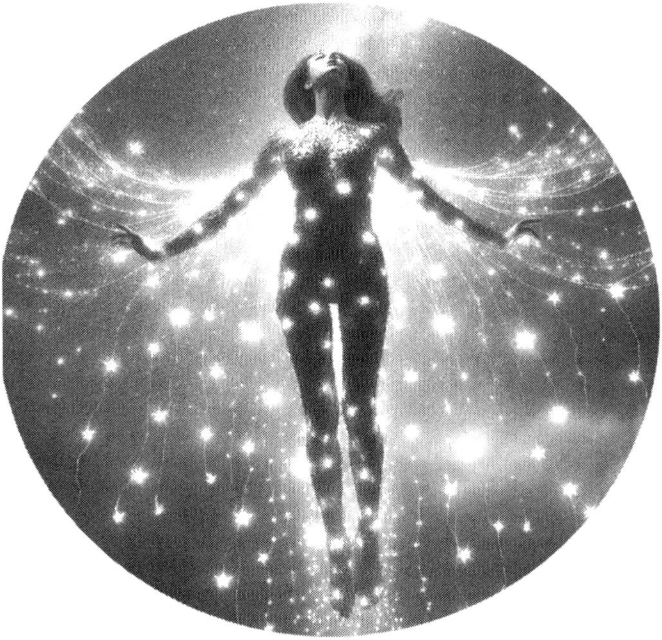

People

Meg Graham Greenwood

Angela's mother and Guy's wife

Guy Greenwood

Angela's father

Angela Greenwood O'Connor

Witch transferred from England to California following her husband, Robin.

Robin/Rob/Robbie O'Connor,

Photographer to the stars and all-round loveable rogue

Anastasia/Anna O'Connor, their daughter

Sean and Paul O'Connor

Robin's twin brothers

Steve Speirs, Al Dean and Don Fargo

Managers of Robin's photographic studios

Nik Chilton

Former boss of Angela's aunt Zella in Los Angeles,

who gave Rob his first chance as a professional photographer.

Sherina/Cam Chilton

Nik's wife, famous jazz pianist, friend of Angela and Lena

Catherine/Katy Chilton

Their daughter, friend of Anna's

Lena Michaels

Friend of Cam Chilton's, has weak witch powers

Sandy and Marcus

Her children

Danny Charlton

World famous music icon, great friend and mentor of Robin

Jill Perkins

Dan's fiancé

Rick Adams

Lead Singer of Robin's favorite band, **Lakota**.

Joe Graham

Meg's half-brother, Angela's uncle, Robin's adopted uncle

Hazel/Zella Brook Graham

Joe's wife

Meggie-Clair/Greta and Jack

Zella and Joe's children

The Veil

The barrier separating the worlds of the living and the dead. "Light as air and stronger than steel". Only very special witches have the ability to pass through at will, although sometimes the dead, sharing the suffering of loved ones, can visit the living in times of distress.

People from beyond the Veil who will pop up from time to time.

Molly Carrick Graham – Angela's maternal great grandmother and Claire's soulmate

Claire Armstrong Graham – Angela's aunt, Joe's mother

Josiah/Josh Greenwood – Angela's paternal grandfather

Robert Graham – Angela's maternal grandfather

Deidra and Dermot O'Connor – Rob's parents

Places

Santa Monica, Pasadena and Huntington Beach

Californian holiday resort towns - locations of Robin's photographic studios.

Santa Barbara - Reina del Sur, Torrance

California homes of Robin and Angela O'Connor.

Ghyll Howe, Nethershaw, Westmoreland, England

Home of Robin's family, where he grew up

Beckton, Westmoreland, England

Home of Angela's family, home of her childhood.

Ghyll Howe, Scarsdale Manor and Bythwaite

Farms owned by the wealthy Greenwood and Graham families in Westmoreland, England.

Smyltandale Cottage (Serenity Vale Cottage)

Home belonging to Angela, a converted mill on the riverbank at Scarsdale, her father's farm.

Millard Falls, Altadena, California
Scene of a death

Lake Arrowhead, San Bernardino, California
Holiday spot of the Chilton family

Linden Reach
Home of the Chilton family

Graham and Greenwood Agricultural Conglomorate Ltd (GGAC)
Situated in Westmoreland and comprising Scarsdale, Bythwaite and Ghyll Howe farms owned by Joe Graham and Guy and Meg Greenwood with Robbie's brothers Sean and Paul stakeholders at Ghyll Howe.

Printed in Great Britain
by Amazon